MW00654420

FORSAKEN TRAIL

USA *TODAY* BESTSELLING AUTHOR

DEVNEY PERRY

FORSAKEN TRAIL

Editing & Proofreading:

Elizabeth Nover, Razor Sharp Editing

www.razorsharpediting.com

Julie Deaton, Deaton Author Services

www.facebook.com/jdproofs

Karen Lawson, The Proof is in the Reading

Judy Zweifel, Judy's Proofreading

www.judysproofreading.com

Cover:

Sarah Hansen © Okay Creations

www.okaycreations.com

OTHER TITLES

The Edens Series

Indigo Ridge

Juniper Hill

Garnet Flats

Jasper Vale

Crimson River

Sable Peak

Christmas in Quincy - Prequel

The Edens: A Legacy Short Story

Haven River Ranch Series

Crossroads

Sunlight

Treasure State Wildcats Series

Coach

Blitz

Rally

Clifton Forge Series

Steel King

Riven Knight

Stone Princess

Noble Prince

Fallen Jester

Tin Queen

Calamity Montana Series

The Bribe

The Bluff

The Brazen

The Bully

The Brawl

The Brood

Jamison Valley Series

The Coppersmith Farmhouse

The Clover Chapel

The Lucky Heart

The Outpost

The Bitterroot Inn

The Candle Palace

Maysen Jar Series

The Birthday List

Letters to Molly

The Dandelion Diary

Lark Cove Series

Tattered

Timid

Tragic

Tinsel

Timeless

Runaway Series

Runaway Road

Wild Highway

Quarter Miles

Forsaken Trail

Dotted Lines

Holiday Brothers Series

The Naughty, The Nice and The Nanny

Three Bells, Two Bows and One Brother's Best Friend

A Partridge and a Pregnancy

Standalones

Clarence Manor

Rifts and Refrains

A Little Too Wild

CHAPTER ONE

ARIA

"Are you here?" August asked.

"Not yet."

"Uhh." He grunted into the phone. "When are you gonna get here?"

"Soon, buddy. I'm about an hour away."

"An hour," he groaned. "That'll take forever."

I laughed. "Go play outside and by the time you build a fairy fort for me to inspect, I'll be there. Now where's your mom?"

"She's sick."

"What?" My spine stiffened. Clara hadn't seemed sick when I'd called last night. "What kind of sick?"

"Um . . . coughing sick? When you get here, can we open my present first?"

"Yes, we can open your present first."

My nephew was five, and I'd missed his birthday. The

1

guilt was real. My attempt to assuage it had resulted in the scooter gift wrapped in the trunk along with a Nintendo Switch game, a puzzle, three books and a remote-control car.

August's birthdays had always been a priority, but I hadn't been able to get away from work this year. Summers were a hectic time at The Gallaway for the head groundskeeper. Toss in my latest duties as fill-in general manager for the luxury hotel on the Oregon coast, and even a quick vacation to see my sister had been impossible.

Normally, Clara and Gus would take a summer trip to my home in Heron Beach for his birthday. Had this been a normal year, we would have celebrated as a family. *August, born in August.* But this year, their trip to Oregon had been moved up to June.

Clara's arrogant and demanding boss had decided that he *needed* his assistant along for his two-week hiatus in Aruba over Gus's birthday.

I couldn't blame Clara for jumping at the lavish vacation. August had turned five in an extravagant, boutique hotel with his favorite person in the world—his mother. They'd gone snorkeling in the ocean and swimming in their suite's private infinity pool. The chef had made Gus's dinner favorite—mini cheeseburgers—then baked him a three-tiered chocolate cake.

Experiencing that moment through Instagram pictures had been depressing.

Maybe we should have partied early for his birthday

during their visit in June, but applauding five when you were stuck at four seemed borderline cruel.

This vacation was my chance to make up for my absence. I was as excited to get to Arizona as August was for me to arrive.

Two weeks with my sister and her son. Two weeks in sweatpants and going barefoot. Two weeks of takeout, games and fun.

"Can you take the phone to your mom?" I asked August.

"Okay. Mom!" he shouted.

I pulled the phone away from my ear and laughed. His feet pounding through their house echoed in the background. After some rustling and mutters, my sister took the phone.

"Hey," she said, her voice muffled and thick.

"Gus said you were sick."

"Ugh." She coughed and sniffled. "I woke up this morning and felt like crap."

"Sorry. I'll be there soon to entertain August so you can get some rest."

"Where are you?"

"About an hour away." I'd worked a half day yesterday to beat the weekend traffic flocking to the coast. I'd pushed hard, spending my Thursday night on the road until I'd finally found a place to stop and a motel room for the night. Then I'd woken up this morning to finish the rest of the twelve-hundred-mile journey, wanting to get to Clara's before dinner.

"Drive safe," she said. "See you when you get here."

"Bye." I ended the call and tossed my phone into my purse in the passenger seat.

Then I gripped the Cadillac's white wheel and relaxed as I floated down the highway.

I loved this car. It was going to break my heart to leave it with Clara in two weeks. But the restored 1964 Cadillac DeVille convertible was not mine to keep. She had been entrusted to me for a short time and soon, she'd continue on her journey to her rightful owner.

But for today, for this trip, she was mine.

The afternoon sun roasted the asphalt. Heat waves rolled across the road, leaving blurry ripples in the air. There were no clouds in the blue sky, nothing to offer relief from the sun's punishing rays. Yesterday I'd spent most of the day with the top down, enjoying the wind in my hair and sunshine on my face. Today I'd keep the top up and the AC cranked.

This heat was the reason I avoided the desert in the summer. By October, it should have cooled, but this year was unseasonably hot.

No wonder everything died here.

Why Clara loved the desert I had no clue. I'd stick with my home on the coast, where the breeze was cool, crisp and freshly salted. Plants and flowers flourished in the ocean air and under the frequent rains.

Life seemed harder here. Nature was unrelenting and only the strong survived. The plateaus in the distance had been eroded into towers and flat-topped spires on the horizon. They'd endured centuries of abuse from wind and water, leaving behind their own unique beauty. The bushes, cacti and wildflowers that managed to thrive were tough as hell. I'd give them credit for their tenacity.

Maybe that was why Arizona appealed to Clara. She was tough as hell too.

The road stretched long and wide ahead. White marking the edges. Yellow the center.

Route 66.

The iconic highway had been mostly empty today, and the stretch ahead was mine and mine alone. I sank deeper into the buttery leather seat and leaned an elbow on the door.

This trip to Arizona wasn't just a trip to visit my twin sister. This trip had a purpose. I was the next driver in a cross-country journey that had started in Boston and would end in California.

This spring, I'd had a surprise visit from an old friend. Katherine Gates had been a welcome sight when I'd spotted her in the lobby of The Gallaway. My childhood friend had traveled from Montana to Oregon. With her and this Cadillac had come memories of the past. Memories I'd locked away for, well . . . too long.

Once upon a time, Katherine and I had lived together.

Our home had been a junkyard. Our family had been a rabble of six runaway teens. We'd been friends. Companions. Protectors.

Katherine.

Londyn.

Gemma.

Karson.

Clara.

Me.

As kids, they'd been the most important people in my life. Then we'd all gone our separate ways, built separate lives, and though I doubted any of us would ever forget the junkyard, time and distance had made it easier to ignore.

When Katherine had surprised me in Oregon, the past had come rushing back. As did my love for my old friends. We were a unit again, the women at least. None of us had been in contact with Karson, not since the junkyard.

But for us girls, we'd rekindled our friendships. Our family.

We had a group text string that more often than not included pictures of wherever we were at the moment. We had video chats to talk about books, though we had yet to talk about books. We had emails and phone calls.

So why, when I had so much love and friendship in my life, was I so lonely?

I clutched the wheel tighter, wishing the hole in my heart away.

The loneliness was probably because I'd been working

so much. And because I'd gone so long without my sister. It would all be better once I got to Arizona, right? Maybe this heavy heart was because I hated goodbyes and soon I'd say farewell to the Cadillac.

God, I was going to miss this car. I would miss all it represented.

The Cadillac hadn't always been a gleaming red classic. Once, it had been Londyn's home, more rust than metal and home to a few mice. Her bedroom had been the backseat. The trunk had served as a closet and pantry. The passenger seat had been the guest room slash living room slash dining room.

What a wonder it was now.

Londyn had started the Cadillac's journey on the East Coast. A flat tire had landed her in West Virginia and in the arms of a handsome mechanic. When Gemma had gone in search of her own fresh start, Londyn had insisted she take the car.

That had been the first handoff.

Gemma had gone to find Katherine at a guest ranch in Montana. Two friends reunited. And two flames. After Gemma had found love, she'd encouraged Katherine to take a trip of her own. Kat had come to find me, and when she'd headed home with her new husband, Cash, it had been my turn with the Cadillac.

Londyn wanted this car to go to Karson, who lived in California, but since I had no desire to return to the Golden State, I was giving the Cadillac's keys to my sister.

One more handoff.

One more trip.

Londyn. Gemma. Katherine. They'd each had their road trip. Mine wasn't as eventful, but it was mine. They'd all found something seated behind the Cadillac's steering wheel. I had no hopes that a car would lead me to the love of my life, but I did hope to find the piece of myself I'd been missing lately.

I'd spent months driving this gorgeous vehicle around Heron Beach. The two-day trip to Arizona was my last hurrah and I was savoring this last hour behind the wheel. Once I arrived at Clara's, there'd be no more driving. I'd fly home in two weeks and get back to work.

Work. I glanced at my phone and debated calling to check in. I dismissed that idea immediately. Before I'd left, Mark, the owner of The Gallaway, had told me to enjoy my well-earned time away. He'd finally brought on a general manager so I could relinquish my temporary command.

Some women, like Gemma and Katherine, wanted to be the boss. They thrived on it. They excelled at it. Not me. All I'd ever wanted was to tend to my plants, watch them grow, and if there was a chance to make a living doing just that, then I was happy.

Especially for The Gallaway. The hotel was a dream.

Before Oregon, Clara and I had lived in Nevada. We'd left the junkyard for the glitz and sparkle of Las Vegas. As two eighteen-year-old girls with nothing to lose, a gamble on Sin City had seemed like a good idea.

I'd lasted a month.

The hotel where I'd worked had been teeming with fake people, both on staff and as guests. So I'd decided Vegas was not my final destination and got busy job hunting. The Oregon coast, where the world was lush and clean, had instantly appealed.

I'd started as a housekeeper at The Gallaway and worked for about a year cleaning rooms. About six months into my employment, I noticed the flowerpots were in need of some pruning. So I came to work early and tackled the blooms, shaping and cultivating them.

One day, the head groundskeeper found me weeding in my maid uniform. He took me under his wing, requesting a transfer from housekeeping to his staff. When he retired, his job became mine.

I worked so The Gallaway overflowed with pink and white flowers in the spring. Peach and purple flourished in the summer. And when the fall came, sprays of yellow and orange and red were everywhere to be seen.

That was the job I wanted. Not management.

But Mark had been good to me, and after the former GM had retired months ago, finding a replacement had been more difficult than expected. Mark had burned through two candidates, one of whom had clearly lied on his résumé and another who'd been a great fit, but her fiancé had proposed one month into her employment and she'd quit to move to Utah.

I crossed my fingers and sent up a silent prayer that this latest hire would stick. Months of doing two jobs had run me dry.

A couple weeks with Clara and August were sure to fill the well.

This drive had filled it some too.

When Clara and Gus had come to Oregon in June, she'd offered to drive the Cadillac home, but I'd insisted on taking it to Arizona myself.

Life had been too stressful. Too frantic. Too busy. This had been my chance to reset and think. I'd never wanted to be the woman who worked endless hours, the woman whose success was defined by the zeros on her paycheck and the title on her business card.

Money was not the end goal of my life.

I focused on the road, my energy spiking with every mile. Today was not the day to kick my own ass for working too hard this summer. Today was for fun and freedom and family.

It took me less than the hour I'd promised August to reach Welcome, Arizona. Rolling down the highway, I took only a brief glimpse at the small town Clara loved. Then I left it in my rearview as I sped toward her home.

A metal security gate greeted me at the driveway entrance. I punched in the code on the keypad and eased down the single lane.

The landscaper had gone for a natural look on the grounds. Mostly rocks and some native shrubs, but there were a few desert willows and velvet mesquite trees to mask the monstrosity at the end of the drive.

Two stories of gleaming glass as sterile and lifeless as the cement walls. Other than a small scrap of green no one could consider a proper front yard, the house was devoid of life, much like the barren and dry landscape that made up the estate.

The modern mansion was only five years old. It had been built around the time August had been born, yet it looked new. It was too clean. Too lonely. It wasn't a home, lived in and loved. It was a showcase. A display of wealth and arrogance.

The house fit its owner.

Broderick Carmichael was all about flash and flaunting his money.

"At least he's not here," I muttered.

It was easy for me to hate the man. Brody had been rude and pompous during our every encounter. How could Clara stand his presence? I'd been asking her that for years without an answer.

When we'd moved to Las Vegas after the junkyard, I'd gone into hospitality while Clara had scoured the classifieds for an office job after getting her GED. She'd started as a receptionist for Brody's company, Carmichael Communications, and had quickly climbed the ranks. When Brody's personal assistant had quit—probably because his boss was spoiled and needy—Clara had been offered the position.

They'd worked together for years. Besides me, Brody was her best friend. Another thing I couldn't make sense of. She was everything he wasn't. Kind. Loving. Compassionate. Clara swore he was all those things, but I wasn't buying it.

When Brody had decided to relocate from the city to this nowhere, tiny town in Arizona—something about a satellite office—he'd offered to bring Clara along. And when he'd built the museum that was his house, he'd also built a small home for Clara and August too. Thank God her house didn't look like its parent.

I turned off the main driveway and parked in front of Clara's garage.

Her home had a modern vibe, like Brody's, but on a subdued scale that rendered the look fresh and simple. The slanted roof allowed for a long bank of windows that overlooked the property. The white siding was clean and bright. The stone accents, along with the plethora of potted succulents and ornamental cacti—my doing—gave it character and color.

Most of the greenery was overgrown from the summer. During my vacation, I'd remedy that with a few hours of trimming and pruning. Clara's only requirement for me when I'd added all of the greenery had been maintenance. She'd water but that was about it.

I put the Cadillac in park, and before I could step out,

the front door to Clara's house burst open and Gus came racing my way.

"Aunt Aria!"

His dark blond hair had grown some since our last FaceTime. His legs looked longer, his face fuller. I'd blinked, and my nephew had changed from a toddler to a boy. He had a dust streak on his cheek and grass stains on his bare knees. He grew too fast.

"Hey!" My heart leapt as I climbed out of the car. I bent, bracing for impact, and scooped him into my arms when he came crashing like a wave. "Oh, I missed you."

"Where's my present?" He squirmed out of my hold, taking in the car.

"August," Clara scolded, coming out the door.

"It's okay." I waved it off and took in my beautiful sister. "Hi."

"Hi." She, like her son, came rushing into my embrace. "We went too long this time."

"I know." I squeezed her tighter.

Normally, we planned five to six visits in a year. Seven if I was lucky. But going four months without seeing them was too long. Work might have kept my mind and body busy, but my heart had paid the price.

A mistake I wouldn't make again.

Clara and August were my only family. We needed each other.

Today maybe more than yesterday.

Clara's nose was red and her cheeks splotchy. Her

pretty brown eyes didn't have their usual sparkle and her shoulders slumped low. She'd trapped her blond hair in a loose ponytail, the ends hanging limp over one shoulder.

"You don't look good."

"I don't feel good." She shrugged and ran a hand over the gleaming hood of the car. "Wow. Look at this thing."

"A beauty, isn't it?"

"I can't believe it's here. That it's my turn." She smiled and stroked the car again. "I love this whole handoff thing."

Clara was a romantic. As teens, she'd buy romance novels for a dime at the thrift store and stay up late reading under the glow of a flashlight. I suspected I'd find a stack of them beside her bed, or a well-stocked Kindle, when I tucked her in for a nap this afternoon.

We'd taken care of each other for the past twenty years. Longer, really. Since our parents had died. We were thirty years old, but that wasn't going to stop me from pampering her while I was here. She'd do the same for me.

"You can gush over the car later. First, we unload. Then, we do presents."

"Yes." Gus did a fist pump.

"And after that, you're taking a long, hot bath followed by a long nap."

Clara gave me a sad smile as exhaustion clouded her pretty face. She looked like she was about to cry.

"What? What is it?" I asked.

"Nothing. I'm just really tired."

I pulled her into my arms again. "Then we'll make sure you get lots of rest."

She collapsed onto my shoulder. "I'm so glad you're here."

"Me too. We both need a vacation, even if yours is at home. No work. Fun only. Just the three of us."

"About that. There's sort of been a change of plan."

I let her go and narrowed my eyes. "What change?"

The whirl of tires and the hum of an engine filled the air before she could answer. A shiny black Jaguar came down the driveway and my heart dropped.

No. That son of a bitch Brody Carmichael was going to ruin my vacation.

"He's supposed to be gone." If he dared encroach on my time with Clara, I'd sneak poison ivy into his bed.

"It's not his fault." Clara sighed, quick to defend her boss.

"Did his private plane not have enough spiced cashews for his liking? Surely he can afford jet fuel."

The second-best part of this week, besides Clara and Gus, was Brody's scheduled absence. Clara knew there was no love lost between me and her boss, so she'd suggested travel dates that coincided with his vacation.

Yet here he was, parking a car that likely cost more than all of my worldly possessions combined.

Brody parked behind the Cadillac and stepped out of his car, sliding the sunglasses off his face. He wore a navy suit tailored to perfection around his broad shoulders and long legs. In the years I'd known him, I'd never seen him in anything but a suit. Did he not own jeans?

"Brody!" August raced over, holding up a hand for a high five. "Aunt Aria is here. We're gonna open my presents."

"I see that." Brody's lips turned up in a smile. Barely.

If the man ever learned how to deliver one properly, actually show some teeth, he'd be devastating. Especially with the dark, trimmed beard he'd grown a few years ago. It gave him a sexy edge. Or it would have, if his perpetually sour mood wasn't such a major turnoff.

He definitely, definitely didn't turn me on. Oh no.

Broderick Carmichael was enemy number one.

One day I hoped to convince Clara to quit her job with Brody and join me in Oregon. The only flaw in my plan was that she loved her job. She loved her boss.

My beautiful, loyal sister had been duped by the devil.

"Hey." Clara waved at Satan incarnate. "How was the flight back?"

The flight back? From where?

"Fine." He shrugged. "Just wanted to stop by and see how you're feeling."

"I'm good," she lied.

"She's sick," I corrected. "And she'll be spending the weekend recuperating."

His jaw clenched but he didn't respond. He simply gave Clara a nod. "Call me if you need anything. See you tomorrow."

"I'll be ready," she said.

Without another word, he ruffled August's hair, then got in his car and disappeared.

I turned on my sister. "Um . . . ready for what?"

"It's nothing. Just a work thing. And I don't have the energy to get into it right now, so how about presents and that nap you mentioned?"

If not for her cold, I would have insisted on answers. But I'd gotten pretty good at ignoring Brody's existence, and Clara deserved a break.

So I did exactly what I'd promised. I hauled in my things and we both cheered as August opened his gifts.

With their living room littered with wrapping paper, I put her to bed and spent the rest of the afternoon and evening entertaining Gus before it was time to put him to bed.

With him tucked in bed, I did the same for my sister, who'd roused around dinner.

"I'm glad you're here." She snuggled into her pillow. "Thanks for watching him."

"My pleasure. Now sleep." I kissed her forehead. "See you in the morning."

She was snoring by the time I eased out of her room and closed the door.

The fading evening light drew me outside to her deck for a few moments alone. I'd stolen Clara's Kindle and uncorked a bottle of wine. As I settled into a lounge chair, I tipped my head to the heavens.

Stars twinkled like diamonds in the midnight sky.

There wasn't a breath of wind. In Oregon, even from my place in town, there was the constant whisper of the ocean's waves. Not here. There was nothing but the occasional screech from a hawk or the scrape of a lizard's claws on a nearby rock.

From my seat, I had the perfect view of Brody's home. It stood dark and endless. The only light came from the second-floor balcony. Maybe if I was lucky, he'd get Clara's cold and be bedridden for a couple weeks.

A girl could hope.

I'd unlocked the Kindle's screen, ready to dive into the tale of a pirate and the fair maiden he'd kidnapped at sea, when something caught my eye.

Brody emerged onto his lit balcony, wearing only a towel wrapped around his narrow hips.

Even from this distance, the definition of his hard stomach was impossible to miss. As was the plane of his wide, bare chest dusted with dark hair. Brody's arms were ropes upon ropes of muscle.

My breath hitched. My pulse quickened. Damn you, Brody Carmichael. Why couldn't he be ugly? It would be so much easier to hate him if he didn't elicit such a strong physical reaction. Undoubtedly, when I dove into my novel, Brody's face would be the pirate's.

His sixth sense must have prickled. One moment, he was leaning, arms braced, on the balcony railing. The next, he stood straight, his hands fisted at his sides, and faced my way.

I gave him a little finger wave and a glare.

I got nothing in return. As quickly as he'd come outside, he vanished inside his concrete castle.

The bastard was probably annoyed that I was here to steal Clara's attention. *Whatever.* These were my two weeks with her. Mine. I was here now, and the loneliness had begun to fade. The well wasn't bone dry.

Four months apart had been too long. Maybe it was time to push harder for a change. Maybe it was time to open my mind to a change of my own.

Clara needed help with August. I simply needed Clara and August. There was a weight on her shoulders that hadn't been there in June, and it had nothing to do with her cold. She was here, working alone. Living alone. Parenting alone.

Enduring alone.

Our lives had been harder than they should have been, harder than my parents had planned. We'd walked a rocky, rough road.

Maybe it was time to switch directions. To forge a beaten path.

And find out if there was a rainbow waiting at the end of my forsaken trail.

CHAPTER TWO

BRODY

"How long will *she* be here?" I asked Clara.

I stood at the floor-to-ceiling-window wall in my office that overlooked the property beyond the house. The office was adjacent to my bedroom, and from here I could see Clara's backyard and deck. I'd designed it that way, wanting to give her privacy but be close enough in case of an emergency. I'd wanted a line of sight.

I was regretting that decision. Just like I had last night when I'd come out for a quiet minute alone, only to realize I hadn't been the only one seeking a moment of solitude.

She had taken over Clara's deck. Last night. Today. She'd brought the old Cadillac. Wasn't it time for her to scurry on back to Oregon?

Outside, Aria was stretched on a chaise with August tucked into her side. The two of them were reading a book, the boy eating up her every word. Her toned legs stretched long to her bare feet. She'd sat in exactly the same chair this morning, painting her toenails.

"Two weeks." Clara sniffled, her voice thick and raspy. "I'm not sure why you're asking me a question when you already know the answer."

I frowned. "Because I was hoping the answer would change."

"Don't." She sighed. "Please. I don't have the energy to play referee."

"What a fucking disaster," I muttered.

Not only had my grandmother's phone call completely disrupted my plans for the next two weeks, forcing me to cancel the trip I'd planned for a year, but now I'd have to be around Aria Saint-James for the next two weeks.

"She's my sister, Brody," Clara said. "She's welcome here. And if you make her feel unwelcome, then I'm moving."

"You can't move." I spun away from the glass. That was the first time she'd ever made that threat, and I didn't like how serious it sounded. "That's your house."

"No, it's *your* house. I just live there."

"Semantics. You're not moving."

Welcome was a safe community with good schools. Selling her on the move here hadn't been difficult for those reasons. Plus a new home with state-of-the-art security. She belonged here. If that meant I had to play nice with the sister, so be it.

"I'll be on my best behavior." I feigned a bow.

"Good. This is an important trip for Aria. I haven't seen her in months, and she's going through something."

"What something?" I asked, forgetting that I didn't care.

"I don't know." Clara dug through the pocket on her hoodie, pulling out a wad of tissues. "She hasn't told me anything, but I can feel it."

Clara and Aria were fraternal twins, similar physically but each with their own unique traits, yet they had a bond like nothing I'd seen before. Their link was one I'd never understand but it existed like the walls, ceilings and floors of this house.

There were days when work was so stressful that Clara reached her wits' end—Aria would always call. There were days when Clara would excuse herself in a meeting—she just had to text Aria. It was like they had a direct tap into each other's moods and knew when the roller coaster had hit a low.

"Can we talk through the plan for tonight? The pilot will be ready to take off any time after five. What time do I need to be ready?" Clara put the tissues to her nose and blew hard. A snot bubble escaped the edge.

"Hell. You can't go tonight."

"Yes, I can."

"You're not going. You look awful."

She pulled the tissues away from her face. "Gee. Thanks. I hope you don't say that to your real dates."

"You know what I mean." I walked to the bathroom off the office and rifled through the cabinet until I found a fresh box of tissues. Then I brought them out to Clara where she'd collapsed on the couch, curled into the fetal position. "Here."

"Thanks." She clutched the box to her chest, her eyelids so droopy she couldn't keep them open.

"Go home. Get some sleep. I'll go solo tonight."

"No way." Clara pushed herself up with a grunt. "I'll be fine. I just need a nap and a shower. Then I'll be good to go."

I sat beside her. "Sorry, but you're not coming. Boss's orders."

"Ha." She laughed, which turned into a fit of coughs. "Since when do I take my boss's orders?"

"Fair point."

Clara relaxed, her body sagging toward mine. I put an arm around her shoulders and held her before she could collapse onto the floor.

It was rare for us to hug. Was this a hug? Clara hugged everyone she knew but I wasn't really the hugging type. But I considered her a friend. A best friend. Or . . . the closest thing I had to a best friend. Did it count when you paid them?

Probably not.

Such was my life. Nannies. Tutors. Chauffeurs. Chefs. All had been friendly. In the early days, I'd confused their smiles and affection for love. But they'd understood what I hadn't as a child.

When the kid was happy, you got to keep your job.

Me being the kid.

After any of the employees assigned to my care had quit or left the Carmichael estate for other opportunities, I'd never heard from them again.

The same would be true with Clara. If she quit and left here, I wouldn't hear from her again.

Finding another assistant like her would be impossible. She had years of experience on my staff. She was organized and efficient. She knew the boundaries between personal and professional. She pushed when necessary but didn't cross the line in the sand.

And she was nice. I liked Clara. She was an easy travel companion. August was a cool kid. I hadn't been around many children, not even when I'd been a child, but he was funny, bright and polite.

Clara was not moving.

I simply wouldn't allow it.

"You should go home," I said. "Get some rest."

She didn't answer.

"Clara?" I bent, taking in her face. Her eyes were closed and her mouth was hanging open. She'd fallen asleep.

"Clara." I gave her a little shake.

"What?" She jerked awake, wiping at her mouth with the back of her hand.

"Go home."

"Okay." She nodded and paused, summoning the strength to stand.

"Here." I threaded my arm under hers and hoisted us both up to our feet. "Can you make it home?"

"Yeah." She slipped free and shuffled across the room, then stopped beside the door. "What time did we decide?"

"No time. You're not going."

"Brody, you shouldn't go alone."

"I can handle this." My family's functions were like swimming with sharks, but it wouldn't be the first time I'd jumped in the water alone. Yes, a date would have been a nice buffer. But it wasn't worth making her miserable.

"You need—" She sneezed, which made her cough. The cough led to a fresh glob of snot shooting out of one nostril. She dove for a tissue, blowing and wiping.

My God, she looked awful.

"You need a date," she said.

"I'll go alone."

"Brody, I'll be fine. I can go. I have the dress and everything. It's the least I can do."

"You're miserable."

"I've survived worse."

She'd survived too much. Occupational hazard of working so closely with each other. Clara knew about my life. I knew the vague details of hers. She was more tight-lipped about her childhood, but I'd been in the front row during the struggles she'd overcome in Las Vegas. Namely, August's father.

If I couldn't be spared from tonight's spectacle, I could at least save Clara from the same fate. "It's a wedding. I've gone to weddings alone before."

"And you hated every minute. This isn't just any wedding."

No, it wasn't. Tonight, my ex-fiancée was marrying another man. The woman I'd once cared for was marrying my younger brother.

"Please, don't go alone. Otherwise . . . oh, never mind."

"Otherwise I'll look sad and alone and pathetic."

She blew her nose. The honk was a resounding yes.

I'd planned to be blissfully absent from the wedding festivities, lounging on my favorite beach in Fiji. Except one phone call from Grandmother and I'd been summoned to attend. No exceptions.

Or she'd sell the company.

"One more year." I sighed. "One more year and she won't be able to pull my strings."

Clara gave me a sad smile. "It will be worth it."

"God, I hope so."

In another year, I'd be thirty-five and the stipulations on my trust would expire. My grandfather had left me a large inheritance after he'd died unexpectedly of a heart attack. Upon my thirty-fifth birthday, the funds would be completely at my disposal. The money would be nice, though I already had plenty, but what I really wanted was full control of the company.

The shares Grandmother controlled on my trust's behalf would also be released on my birthday.

Coreen Carmichael was about to lose her grip on my leash, much to her dismay because Grandmother loved nothing more than to manipulate her grandsons. Especially me.

My attendance at this wedding had been *requested*, according to the email her assistant had sent Clara. Requested meaning required. So though I'd been halfway across the world, I'd informed the pilot that there'd been a change of plan and we'd turned around to head home.

"Let's think of alternatives." Clara pushed away from the door and returned to the couch, plopping down on its edge. Her sweats bagged on her frame, the hems pooling at her ankles and the slippers she'd worn over here this morning. "What about Marie? The girl you dated a few months ago."

"No." I crossed my arms and perched on the edge of my desk. Clara didn't know the details, but Marie was more likely to cut my throat than agree to a date. She'd been angry, to say the least, when I'd dumped her after she'd told me she was in love with me. Maybe another man would have let her down gently, but I'd only been seeing her for three weeks. We'd gone on four dates.

Marie had loved my billions. Not me.

"I could call some friends from my yoga class," Clara said. "There are a few single women who'd probably go."

"I'm not taking a blind date." That sounded more torturous than the wedding itself.

Clara chewed on her bottom lip. "Yeah, you're right. You need someone who knows this is only supposed to *look* like a date."

"This is business."

She nodded. "Then that only leaves us one choice."

"You're not go—"

"You have to take Aria." We spoke in unison.

I blinked. "Pardon?"

"Aria. You have to take Aria. We can explain to her what's going on. She'll be able to act as a buffer and keep the vultures at bay. You won't look sad and alone and pathetic. It's actually better than if I were to go with you. She'll look like an actual date, not your assistant."

Was she serious? This had to be the cold medicine talking. She was delusional if she thought I'd actually take her sister. "No."

"This is perfect." Her face lit up and some of the weight came off her shoulders.

"No."

"She's my size, so she can wear my dress."

"No."

"You need to leave here around five. The flight to Vegas is less than an hour but there might be traffic. I don't want you to be late."

"No."

"The wedding starts at seven, right?"

"No."

Her forehead furrowed. "It doesn't? I could have sworn the invite said seven. I have it on my desk. I'll double-check when I get home."

"Yes, it starts at seven. But no, I'm not taking Aria."

"Why not?"

"Because . . . I don't like Aria."

Her mouth pursed into a thin line.

"She doesn't like me either."

Clara huffed. She knew I was right.

There had never been a minute, a second or a fraction of a second that Aria and I had gotten along. The first time we'd met had been in Vegas, not long after I'd hired Clara as my new assistant. Aria had come to visit and Clara had wanted to show off her new office, so she'd brought Aria in for a tour.

At first, I mistook her for the weekend cleaning crew. I didn't notice the similarities in her features to Clara's. After Aria corrected me, I took maybe ten minutes out of their precious visit, ten fucking minutes, to run through a to-do list with Clara. Apparently, my business annoyed Aria. I'd infringed on *her* time. She had the gall to snap at me. In my own goddamn office. She had the nerve to tell me that Clara was off the clock and my precious demands would have to wait.

No one told me what to do, certainly not in my own building.

So I told her that if she didn't like it, I could arrange for her to be flown home. Immediately.

That was one of the tamest exchanges we'd had over the years.

During one visit here, she'd walked through Clara's new house and made a list of improvements. The deck—three inches off the ground—needed a railing. The front door—of a house guarded by motion sensors and a gate—didn't have a deadbolt. The staircase should have a baby gate and the cupboards needed safety latches—for a baby who couldn't so much as roll over.

The list went on for two pages. Not wanting to burden Clara with the task, Aria marched it over, threw it in my face and told me that if I had enough money to build my monstrosity of a house, I could at least make sure Clara's cottage was safe for an infant.

Just thinking about it made my nostrils flare.

Last year, Clara had gone to Oregon to visit Aria during the summer. I called a few times, four tops, to check in. On my last call, Aria answered. She'd stolen Clara's phone to inform me that if I couldn't fuck off for the five days, she'd throw Clara's phone in the ocean.

And Clara thought we should attend a wedding together? That we could convince people we were a couple? Ludicrous. Aria and I would kill each other before the cocktail hour was over.

No, tonight I needed an ally by my side. Not a woman who thought I was a "demanding prick."

Maybe I did rely on Clara too much. That was Aria's hang-up. But Clara was the only person in this world I trusted. She was the only one I believed, without a shadow of a doubt, was on my side.

The employees at Carmichael Communications were loyal, but my grandmother emitted a strong sphere of influence.

Coreen was a master manipulator. She wove a dangerous web. Grandmother had a knack for making people feel special. Cherished. You trusted her faithfully, right up until that moment when she shoved a dagger between your ribs.

It was part of the reason I'd moved to Welcome: to escape Vegas and her pit of vipers. Here, I could do my work with minimal interference. On a good day, I spoke to her once. And here, I could run my own businesses, the ones she had no part in, while I bided my time.

Fifty-four weeks and three days.

Then I'd be thirty-five.

Then Carmichael would be mine.

When that day came, I needed Clara by my side. The last thing I needed was to strangle her sister at a wedding.

"I'm not taking Aria."

"Then I'll go." Clara sighed and stood.

"I'll go alone."

She walked to the door, ignoring me completely. "See you at five."

I waited until I heard the front door open and close. "No, you won't."

I'd leave here at four. By the time she wandered over, I'd be gone. And then she'd have no choice but to go home and rest.

It was just a wedding. I'd be fine alone, right?

This evening would be enough of a headache with my own family. I wasn't adding Clara's sister to the mix.

Fuck. Grandmother was a sick woman for making me go tonight. I rubbed a hand over my face and returned to the window.

And there she was. Aria. Still on the deck.

She'd traded her seat in the chair for a seat on the deck boards. Her legs were crossed as she and August bent over a toy. It looked like a car of some sort. Probably one of her presents. Gus loved remote-controlled toys so it wouldn't surprise me if he'd requested one from his aunt as a birthday gift.

I'd given him an actual ride-in Jeep. It always made me smile when I stood at the glass and watched him exploring his driveway and yard. There wasn't much for greenery around my house, but Clara's looked like a tropical paradise compared to the barren desert beyond the yard fence.

Aria's doing, no doubt. This morning, when I'd had

my coffee, she'd been out with watering can and shears, pruning the pots and planters.

She was a gorgeous woman.

Much to my dismay, her looks always made my heart beat a bit faster. Just my type too. Beautiful. Obstinate. Bold. Aria's looks were different than Clara's, though they shared some features. The pretty bows of their lips. The tips of their noses. The same shining brown eyes flecked with gold. And a realism for life beyond their years.

Clara and Aria were four years my junior, having recently turned thirty, but they carried themselves with wisdom gained from experience, not age. Maybe that was why Aria disliked me so. On day one, she'd looked me up and down and found me lacking.

She wasn't alone.

Grandmother would probably love her. An image of them sitting together at the wedding popped into my head. They were laughing and drinking champagne as they kibitzed about my shortcomings and former vices. Women. Cars. Booze. Gambling.

Ten years ago, they would have been right. Ten years ago, I'd been young and impulsive. I'd thrown my money around like discount candy at a parade. But a lot had changed in a decade. I'd grown up. I'd made mistakes and learned from them. I'd been betrayed and learned from that too.

Still, when she looked at me, she saw my father.

Her son-in-law.

The man who'd corrupted her precious daughter. The man who'd spent her millions. The man who'd abandoned his own last name to assume hers.

At least he wouldn't be there tonight. Grandmother couldn't summon him or my mother from their graves. To this day I wasn't sure if she'd been hurt by their deaths or if she was simply mad that death had stolen her puppets.

Clara and Aria had lost their parents in a drunk driving accident. The same way I'd lost mine, only my parents had been the drunk drivers.

On the deck, Aria laughed, throwing her head to the sky as August shot to his feet, the car in his hand, and ran to the grass. He raced it in swerves and circles across the lawn while his aunt watched on, clapping and cheering.

A gorgeous woman.

Her hair was darker than Clara's. Both had dyed their natural dirty-blond shade. Clara had always gone for highlights, accentuating the blond. Aria's seemed to get darker with each visit to Arizona. Today it hung in chocolate waves, messy and sexy, down to the middle of her back.

Her arms were lean but strong, her legs long and firm. She had the body of a woman who knew how to work and wasn't afraid to meet the day head-on. There was no priss to Aria Saint-James. Nothing fake or plastic.

The exact opposite of every woman who'd be in attendance tonight. Especially the bride. I grinned, imagining Heather's face if I strolled into her wedding with a beautiful woman like Aria on my arm.

Revenge wasn't best served cold. It worked best when dripping with sex and superiority.

Maybe Clara had been on to something. Maybe—

No. Hell no.

Aria loathed my existence. And not even Clara held enough sway over her sister to get her to agree to be a wedding date.

Aria's gaze turned toward my house. The wind caught a lock of her hair and blew it into her mouth, so she tugged it away.

There was no way for her to see through the mirrored glass, but the way she stared, the way her eyes narrowed, was like she could see me watching. She wordlessly scolded me for intruding on her time with Gus.

So I backed away from the window and retreated to my desk, where I spent a few hours returning emails and phone calls, watching the clock tick down. The pit of dread in my gut grew deeper by the minute.

Jesus, I hated my family.

My grandmother. My brother. My soon-to-be sister-in-law. I hated them all. I hated their friends. I hated their colleagues. I hated that tonight they'd see me alone. Vulnerable.

Because besides my paid employee, who else did I have?

When time ran out, I hurried through a shower, then donned my best tuxedo, the black Italian fibers having been tailored specifically for my frame. I knotted a solid black tie at my neck and fastened my diamond cufflinks. And with my Patek Philippe watch around my wrist, I snagged the Jaguar's keys from the table beside the door and made my way to the driveway where my butler, Ron, had parked it this morning after having it detailed and waxed.

Stepping outside, I filled my lungs with the clear desert air. I wouldn't get another fresh breath until I returned home. Las Vegas would stick to me like gum under a shoe, unwelcome and a damn mess to clean.

The cooler temperatures of Arizona suited me fine. In the summer, it was warm. In the fall, the nights cooled and made life bearable.

My shoes clicked on the concrete as I made my way toward the driveway. The weight of the keys in my palm kept my hand from shaking. The other, I tucked into a pocket.

One night.

All I had to do was make it through this one night. Then one more year, two weeks, and three days.

Before Thanksgiving of next year, I'd be a free man. No longer bound by the wishes of a dead man. Trapped by the whims of his wife.

I sucked in one more fortifying breath and rounded the corner, only to stop short at the sight of my car.

And the woman standing beside it.

She huffed. "It's about damn time."

CHAPTER THREE

ARIA

"Thanks for opening the door," I deadpanned as Brody rounded the hood of his Jag. "Such a gentleman. Do you treat all your dates with such attention?"

"You're not my date."

"I didn't get dressed up for nothing." I motioned to the emerald gown Clara had conned me into earlier.

The dress was cut low in front, past my breastbone in a deep V. The back dipped beneath my shoulder blades. The satin clung to my torso before flaring out at the hips, billowing into a skirt that swished around my legs. For a woman who'd never had a prom, this dress was as fancy as I'd ever been.

Clara had taken one look and declared the dress had been made with me in mind. Then she'd watched me like a hawk from outside the bathroom, ensuring that I was doing my best primping work.

Her makeup stash had been properly raided and her curling iron thoroughly misused. My eyes were lined and my cheeks were rosy. My hair was curled and hung loosely down my back. She'd tucked a jeweled pin into one side, pulling a section away from my temple. The pin's stones matched the gown's color to perfection.

I'd spent more time on my appearance today than I had in the past year.

Brody shot me a look from over the top of the car, then he opened the driver's side door.

"Seriously? You're not even going to open my door." I gripped the handle and yanked it open with too much force.

"No." He shook his head. "You're not going."

"That gruff, bossy tone doesn't work on me." I gave him a saccharine smile. "I don't work for you."

"What did Clara tell you?"

I lifted a shoulder. "She begged me to be your date to some ostentatious wedding. She promised there'd be champagne. And she promised you'd be nice."

"He will be nice!" Clara shouted as she walked down the driveway with August at her side. The shout made her dissolve into a fit of coughs.

"You should be resting," Brody and I said at the same time.

I scowled at him, then turned it toward my sister. "Go inside."

She waved me off, coughing as she neared the car. "I'm fine. August is going to take care of me after you guys leave. Isn't that right, bud?"

His chest puffed up. "Yep. We're ordering pizza for dinner."

"Pizza," I moaned. I loved pizza. "There's no chance this wedding will be catered by Domino's, is there?"

Clara giggled. "None."

"Didn't think I'd get lucky."

"You can stay for pizza," Brody said. "Because you're not going."

If the man didn't want me along, fine. I wasn't going to force it. I'd already done my best by showing up, dressed to perfection and wearing a pair of toe-pinching heels. What more could I do? I knew when I wasn't welcome. And avoiding an evening with Brody was no hardship.

I opened my mouth, ready to accept defeat, but my beautiful, red-nosed and stuffed-up sister spoke first.

"She's going." Clara leveled her gaze on Brody. "Don't be an idiot. You and I both know this is the best option. Besides, look at her."

"What about me?" I dropped my gaze to my feet.

"You're beautiful," Brody admitted through clenched teeth. It sounded pained, like it was either admit that I looked good—because I looked *good*—or have a tooth pulled without anesthesia.

"Gee. Thanks." I rolled my eyes.

"Heather will hate it." Clara gave Brody an evil grin.

Who was Heather? My darling sister had skipped over some details in her rushed explanation as to why I was going. Because that gleam in her eyes was nothing more than petty spite.

I could get behind petty spite, as long as I knew who we were spiting.

Brody pondered her words, his jaw clenched and his stare impassive. "Shit."

"Brody said a bad word." August pointed at Brody and looked up to Clara, waiting for his mother to take action.

"Yes, he did." Clara cocked a hip and shot her boss a sideways look.

"Sorry. Dam-darn." He sighed and left the car, walking over to August. He dug in his pocket and came out with a quarter, handing it to my nephew. "Piggy bank."

"Yes." August fist-pumped and grinned at me.

I gave him a wink.

August had four piggy banks, more than any kid needed, but each had a purpose. One was for his birthday money. One was for money he found himself, like pennies and dimes discarded on sidewalks. The third was for his weekly allowance. Clara paid him five dollars a week to make his bed each morning and pick up his toys at night. And the fourth, the most recent addition, was for money he took off Brody and occasionally

Clara when one of them slipped and swore in his presence.

Last night when he'd given me the full tour of his room, showing me everything new he'd acquired since my last visit, he'd made sure to give each of the banks a hefty shake.

The bad-word piggy had by far the most change.

"Okay, kid." Brody gave August a fist bump. "I'd better get out of here. I'm all out of quarters."

"Or you could stop saying bad words," I said.

That comment earned me a death glare over his shoulder, but when he touched the tip of August's nose, it was with a warm, genuine smile. Brody's affection for August was his only redeeming quality.

That, and the way he looked in a tux.

Even I had to admit he looked delicious. The suit wrapped around his broad shoulders and encased his strong arms. His slacks molded to his thick legs and muscled behind. The trimmed beard added a rough edge to his otherwise smooth, classy appearance. And the tie . . . I wasn't going to admit that I wanted to untie it with my teeth.

He was infuriating and arrogant. But damn . . . there were very adult words and scenarios running through my mind. If August had any clue what I was thinking, I'd fill that piggy bank to its ears.

My cheeks flushed. A flare of desire coursed through my veins. Any other man, and I'd be a puddle of lust by the end of the night. But this was Brody. All I had to do was wait until he opened his mouth to speak and he'd turn me off entirely.

"Have fun," Clara said as Brody returned to the driver's side of his car.

"Not likely," I muttered.

"Then have . . . er"—she looked between the two of us —"safe travels."

"Save me some pizza," I said when she came over for a hug.

Clara was a hugger. She hugged her hellos. She hugged her goodbyes. She hugged everything in between. When we'd split apart, it was the one thing I'd missed most. Conversations we could have over the phone, but they were no replacement for a rib-cracking hug.

I'd found myself giving more hugs when she wasn't around, simply because I'd missed them from her.

"Thank you for doing this," she whispered.

"For you? Anything." I let her go and waved goodbye to August.

I slid into the car, surprised to find the leather seat cool to the touch. Someone had come out here and started the engine to let the air-conditioning run. I rolled my eyes. It wasn't even that hot outside, but heaven forbid Brody break a sweat.

He climbed in behind the wheel, but he didn't pull out of the drive. "Why are you doing this?"

"Because Clara asked me to."

Beyond the windshield, my sister took August's hand and the two of them walked down the driveway toward their house. She was still in her sweats from this morning. Her hair was a mess and her eyes tired. But she hid it as best she could for her son. She smiled and swung his hand beside her hip, taking him home, where they'd probably cuddle on the couch watching cartoons until it was pizza time.

"You hate me," Brody said.

When I turned to face him, his green eyes were waiting.

Brody's eyes were the first thing I'd noticed about him years ago. They were disarming. They were almost too bright to be real. The green was a spiral of shades from lime to hunter. It was all held together by a ring of sable around the iris. They always reminded me of a patch of creeping Jenny snaking its way through moss on a summer day.

"Yes, I do." I hated Brody. I'd been hating him for years. "But I love Clara more than I hate you. Apparently, this wedding is important. And if I didn't go, she would have."

He blew out a deep breath, facing forward. "It is. Important."

"Then let's go."

He shoved the car in gear and roared down the asphalt, racing for the gate, like if he didn't get us off his property this instant, he'd change his mind.

I held my breath, fighting the urge to let my knees bounce. I'd seen plenty of weddings at The Gallaway. I often worked with florists in the area to tie the exterior flowers into centerpieces for the event. But this was different. I wasn't going to stay in my tennis shoes and tee, lurking in the dark corners and appreciating the show from a distance.

Tonight, I was a guest. I'd never been to a wedding as a guest. When I'd admitted that truth to Clara, she'd told me not to tell Brody.

No problem there. I doubted we'd share a lot of conversation.

I was arm candy, not entertainment.

The drive to the Welcome airport was uneventful. Silent. Though the air-conditioning was cranked, the heat won the battle. It seeped off Brody's large frame as tension radiated from his shoulders.

When he pulled into the airport, I expected him to park in the parking lot and lead me through the small terminal. Silly me. Brody was no mortal man. He drove straight for the runway. With the planes.

He parked beside a jet that gleamed silver and white under the Arizona sun. Its windows sparkled like those diamonds he had on his cuffs.

I'd never owned a diamond. Hell, I'd never even touched a diamond.

An attendant opened my door and extended a hand to help me from the car.

"Thanks," I breathed and steadied my feet.

The wealth was staggering. Maybe I'd gotten in a bit over my head because—*no freaking way*—there was a carpet leading to the plane. Gray, not red, but a freaking carpet nonetheless.

"Madam." The attendant bowed. He actually *bowed*.

He was older, likely in his fifties, with white streaked liberally through his blond hair. He carried a halo of sophistication, and even though his blue eyes were kind and welcoming, he knew I wasn't here by my own free will.

My sweet, sweet sister was going to owe me big-time.

I opened my mouth to tell him the bow wasn't necessary—I wasn't the queen—but he bowed again, this time to Brody.

"Sir. We're ready."

"Thank you, Ron." Brody tossed the man his keys, then strode toward the plane, taking the stairs without a backward glance my way.

"Oh, you're such a jackass," I muttered under my breath, glowering at Brody's shoulders. Then I hiked up my gown's billowing skirt and hurried to catch up. Stiletto heels were not my specialty and I teetered on the last step before emerging inside the airplane's cabin.

Leather and citrus filled my nose. Cool air rushed over my skin.

The plane was nothing but golden light and cream finish. Every surface was polished, every comfort ready at your fingertips. This plane cost more than my entire life. It wasn't the cold, modern style of Brody's home.

This was . . . lush.

No wonder Clara hadn't hesitated to tag along on a tropical vacation.

I'd always thought Mark Gallaway was the richest man I'd ever met. Clearly, I'd underestimated Brody. His house was enormous and state-of-the-art, but this was grand. This was affluence passed down from generation to generation. And the plane seemed more indicative of his wealth than his home or his car.

Had Brody been downplaying his money? That seemed so . . . unlike him. He'd always seemed like the type to flaunt his millions. He *did* flaunt his millions. Except maybe he'd been holding back.

Maybe millions were actually billions.

Brody was in a chair, sipping a glass of water with a lemon wedge, as his fingers flew across the screen of his phone. Probably texting Clara to tell her this was a horrible idea. I was going to do the same as soon as I pulled my phone from my black clutch.

"Madam." Another attendant appeared at my back, bowing again. This one was younger than Ron and his bow not quite as graceful or practiced.

"Aria. Not madam."

"Aria," he corrected with another bow. "May I get you a refreshment?"

"Water. Please."

"Of course."

Before I caught him in another bow, I walked down the aisle and took the seat across from Brody's. "Who's Heather?"

"My ex-fiancée." His attention stayed focused on the phone.

"Ahh. And she'll be at the wedding."

"Yes," he said flatly. "She's the bride."

"Oh," I murmured as the attendant appeared with my water glass balanced perfectly on a black tray. I took it, cringed at yet another bow—*please, stop bowing*—and waited until he'd disappeared behind a curtain toward the cockpit. "Tell me what I'm getting into here."

Brody scowled but tucked his phone into the jacket pocket of his tux. "My ex-fiancée, Heather, is marrying my brother, Alastair."

"Did she become his fiancée before or after she was no longer yours?"

"Before. During. Neither will admit they'd been fucking before the one time I caught them in the act, but I know Alastair and he's never been one to abstain."

"Alastair." My nose scrunched. "And I thought Broderick was pretentious."

"They are family names."

"Shocking." The word dripped with sarcasm.

That type of retort would normally incense Brody. It should have antagonized him into some verbal sparring. At the very least, that blatant censure should have earned me a glare and a jaw tic.

Instead . . . nothing. His gaze was unfocused as he stared ahead, like he'd missed my comment entirely. Brody's fingers tapped on his knee.

Was he nervous? The signs were subtle, so much so that most would probably miss them. But I knew Brody. He always fought for the last word. Always.

Like he always fought back.

"She left you for your brother, right? Heather?"

He nodded, his eyebrows coming together, but that gaze was still locked on some imaginary spot on the plane's wall.

Interesting. Clearly, I was along as revenge of sorts. Did he still love her? How painful would this be for him?

Or maybe his fears had nothing to do with the bride. Maybe his fears were because I was on his arm instead of my sister.

"I won't embarrass you," I promised.

Brody blinked and mentally replayed my words. And when his gaze met mine, it was softer than I'd ever seen it before. He looked at me the way he looked at Clara. With kindness. "That's not what I'm worried about."

"Are you sure?"

"My family is . . . difficult. I avoid them mostly. The last place I want to be is at this wedding, but I have no choice."

That was all the explanation I got. The attendant

entered the cabin, his hands clasped behind his back. "We'll be leaving momentarily, sir."

"Very good," Brody said, dismissing him.

The pilot greeted us next, outlining the details of the flight and shaking Brody's hand. They all called him sir. Everywhere we'd gone tonight, he was *sir*.

It wasn't until we were in the air, the short forty-five-minute flight well underway, that I spoke again. "Clara doesn't call you sir."

"Why would she?"

"Everyone else does."

"Hmm." He hummed and drank the last swig of his water. "She's never called me sir."

Because Clara was different. His relationship with her was different.

And that relationship was the reason the man grated on my every nerve.

I'd first met Brody at his office in Las Vegas. Clara had been so proud of her new job and had wanted to show me her workspace. I'd been proud of her too. She'd built a career in no time flat. She'd climbed out of the junkyard and made something of her life.

Brody had been a budding entrepreneur, or so she'd called him. She'd gushed about his brilliance and creativity and drive. Maybe she'd set the bar too high.

Because the day she took me to the office, he was there too. Clara left me at her desk outside his office to run to the bathroom. The two of us had been guzzling water like thirsty camels after hitting an outlet mall before coming to the office.

Brody's office door was open and when he spotted me, the smug bastard told me that the cleaning staff was not to come in until after eight at night. When I corrected him, informing him that I was Clara's sister, he waved me away. He actually said *shoo*. What kind of asshole said *shoo*?

I stood fuming outside his door, listening as he picked up the phone and ordered someone to buy him a new car. A Ferrari. Whatever model was the most expensive.

By the time Clara returned from her pee break, I was disgusted. Brody then sent her home with a list of tasks to complete when he'd known damn well that she was on an approved vacation.

First impression? Mega douche.

Over the years, he'd done little to change my opinion. Mostly I hated how he spent money. He tossed it around like it was meaningless because Brody had never gone hungry.

Cars. Trips. Homes. Planes. Brody was rich. Did he appreciate it? Did he realize how lucky he was?

Clara promised he was a good man. Was he?

Brody doted on her. He provided for her because he wasn't stupid. He knew she was one of a kind. Clara was the fleck of true gold in a sea of pyrite.

I was the lesser twin, something he liked to remind me of as often as possible.

Once, he'd told Clara that the flowers beside her front

door were gaudy and overgrown. I'd been standing right beside her.

For Clara. I was doing this for Clara. I'd fake a smile through this wedding. I'd drink a lot of champagne and enjoy what she promised would be a five-star meal. Then I'd climb back into my sweats and enjoy the next two weeks with family.

With any luck, Brody would hop back on this very plane and disappear for the rest of my vacation. We'd learned to avoid each other, mostly to spare Clara from being in the middle.

One night of pretending.

Then we'd go back to what we were good at.

Hating.

City lights twinkled in the distance, glowing outside the window. "Ugh. I hate Vegas."

"You and me both," Brody said, his gaze aimed out the small window. "When was the last time you were here?"

"When August was born. I came to help Clara. I offered to help her move too but you took care of that before I could get here."

"Are you really upset? I thought you would have wanted her away from *him.*"

Him. Devan. August's father.

At the time, it had surprised me when Brody had asked Clara to accompany him to Welcome. Maybe he'd known how badly she'd needed to escape Vegas too.

"In that, we can agree. She's better off without Devan in their lives."

Clara had cut Devan loose when August had been a newborn. The two of them had dated for about a year when she'd gotten pregnant. It hadn't been planned. She'd tried to keep him involved, but by the third trimester, he'd already checked out. Knowing that he'd never make a good father—and knowing that she'd never succeed if she tried to change him—she'd given him an out.

He'd signed over his rights to August without hesitation.

Not long after, Brody had approached her with an offer that had been irresistible. A fresh start. A new town. All expenses paid.

"I wanted her to move to Oregon," I said. "I lobbied hard for it."

"Not hard enough." He gave me that smug, cunning grin. The one he always cast my way whenever he won.

"It's hard to compete against a free house, a free car and a free life."

"It's not free. Clara has earned it."

"Even Clara knows she hasn't."

"What do you mean?"

I rolled my eyes. "Why do you think she works so hard for you? Why do you think she would have come to this wedding tonight, sick as a dog?"

He blinked.

Yep. Clueless. "She's trying to balance the scales. You

helped her out of a bad situation with Devan. She wanted to get out of Vegas and leave him behind. Then she came to Arizona and you'd gone so . . . overboard."

He lifted his chin. "I did what I would have done for any other employee."

"Bullshit. Be honest with yourself, Brody. You wouldn't have done that for any other employee. You treat her differently."

"No, I don't. I provide a life for Ron. He has a house on the property too."

"Okay, then why does Ron call you sir but Clara doesn't? I'm guessing she did once, a long time ago, and you told her not to. Because you treat her differently."

His forehead furrowed and there was that jaw tic.

Point for Aria. That round was mine. "There's a fine line between helping someone and making them feel like a charity."

"I don't pity Clara," Brody snapped. "And she knows it."

"Maybe. But the next time you tell her to jump, think about why she asks *how high.* Make sure you aren't taking advantage of my sister's work ethic and the fact that she'll bend over backward for you, all because what you've given her, she has no chance to repay."

He stared at me, shock etched on his handsome face. In his glass tower, he'd never stopped to ask himself *why.*

"We're beginning our descent, sir," the pilot said over the intercom, ending our conversation.

There was a wedding we had to attend.

There was a show for us to put on. Fitting that we were in Las Vegas.

As the plane dipped and headed for the runway, my nerves spiked. Adrenaline and anxiety grew. Rolling. Compounding. Like a snowball flying down a hill, getting bigger and bigger with each spin.

The plane's wheels skidded on the tarmac. The crew in the plane hurried to prepare for our departure, the crew outside for our arrival, red carpet included. When we stepped outside and into the Vegas heat, I groaned. There was no way I'd survive this sober.

"I'm going to need champagne," I told Brody as he led the way to a limo.

Lots and lots of champagne.

CHAPTER FOUR

BRODY

"Good evening." The man stationed at the entrance nodded as we strolled through the door, following the line of guests filing into the reception hall.

Aria clutched my arm as her ankle rolled for the third time. Heels were not her forte, as she'd informed me in the limo. She'd threatened to chuck the shoes and go barefoot if I didn't have an arm available at all times to keep her steady.

"How long will this take?" Aria asked, casting a look over her shoulder to the exit.

"You know how these things drag."

"No, actually, I don't. Enlighten me."

"This is the reception. It will start with cocktails and hors d'oeuvres. Toasts. Then a dinner, likely five or six courses, so it won't be quick. Cake. Toasts. Dancing. More toasts." For each event, Heather would likely have a different dress. "If we're home before dawn, it will be a miracle."

"What about the actual wedding?"

"The ceremony is over." Thank God, I'd missed it. "Heather and Alastair had a private ceremony a few hours ago with close friends and family. Invite only. I didn't get one."

"You're his brother."

"Family doesn't mean the same thing in mine as it does in yours."

She hummed and gripped my arm tighter as we approached the ballroom doors. The pace slowed as people stood in the reception line. My stomach knotted tighter with each inch forward. Then there they were. The happy, cheating couple.

I'd avoided them since the day I'd caught them humping in Heather's apartment. I'd gone over to pick up a watch I'd left there the night before. Surprise. Engagement over.

That day, I'd gone back to work and assigned Clara the task of changing the locks to my penthouse. I'd also decided it was time to move while applauding my foresight to never let Heather move in. She probably would have screwed Alastair in my own damn bed.

Heather's billowing white gown caught my eye first. The cackle of her laugh stabbed my eardrums. Alastair looked so much like my father, there were times when it was difficult to look at his face. His dirty-blond hair was combed to precision, his nose straight and his dimpled chin raised.

He and Dad were alike in more than just looks. Alastair had inherited Dad's greed and gluttony and gullibility. Thankfully, I'd taken after Grandfather. I'd inherited his common sense and work ethic. His brain. Though Grandmother liked to remind me that I was more like my mother than I wanted to admit. Foolish. Impulsive. Driven by emotion.

After all, Mom's biggest weakness, my father, was the reason she was dead.

It was a blessing Mom wasn't here. Toward the end of her life, she'd hated these spectacles as much as I did. But oddly enough, seeing Heather and Alastair together didn't bother me like I'd expected. They deserved one another. When I looked at them, smiling and preening, I felt nothing other than annoyance because they'd ruined a perfectly good Saturday night.

"Her dress is gaudy and hideous," Aria said as we emerged through the threshold of the double doors.

The couple in front of us gaped and sent her horrified looks.

Aria simply smiled. "Hello."

I fought a laugh. It was . . . surprising. I hadn't thought I'd have to fight much other than my gag reflex tonight.

Gaudy was definitely Heather's style. The skirt of her dress ballooned to nearly four feet in diameter. Alastair had to stretch his arm over the skirts to touch his new bride's arm.

Golden light bathed us from head to toe as we shuffled deeper into the ballroom. Crystal sconces cast gleaming rays onto the blue and cream filigree–papered walls. My shoes sank into the lush navy carpet swirled with varying shades of sandstone, powder and ivory.

Islands of cocktail tables covered in white cloths filled the room. A string quartet was playing in the distant corner.

Ornately carved sills framed the windows that lined the room in steady succession. The domed ceiling was broken into sunken sections, each delimited by more carvings and accentuated with chandeliers. The circular ballroom provided a stunning view of the city lights beyond.

"Wow." Aria's eyes roved from wall to ceiling to floor to window. "Quite the place."

"It's something." When Heather had pitched it as the venue for our wedding, I'd nixed it immediately because this was most definitely not me.

"How do you want me to play this?" Aria whispered.

"I . . ." The words died on my tongue. I had no fucking clue. "You tell me. This is my first fake date."

"Same." She straightened. "Let's put on a good show."

This time, I let the smile go free. I glanced down and Aria's pretty brown eyes were waiting. They were flecked with honey and sangria. The reds and yellows were so slight, they swirled into the iris, mixing with the chocolate to give it fire. Aria's fire.

Did Clara have eyes like that? If she did, I hadn't noticed. Why hadn't I noticed? We'd spent more time together than I had with anyone else in a decade.

After only hours in Aria's company, I'd picked up details that I shouldn't have noticed. Like the pout of her lower lip. The delicate lobes of her ears. And now the mesmerizing color in her eyes.

It unnerved me more than seeing Heather and Alastair after all these years.

Aria gave me a small smile, but as we took another step, it changed. Twisted. The fire in her gaze sparked even brighter. The mischievous woman whose words cut like a samurai sword was ready for the show.

Her hand let go of my arm to slide down the sleeve of my tux jacket. Aria laced her fingers with mine as her other hand snaked up my chest. She inched so close that her scent, floral and sweet, filled my nose.

That intoxicating smell scrambled my brain and I couldn't tear my eyes away from the curls in her shiny hair. I wanted to twist them around my fingers, then take the strands in my fist and—

What. The. Fuck.

This was Aria. A woman who openly admitted she hated me the way I hated her. An enemy. My assistant's sister.

There'd be no fisting of her hair. No licking of her lips. No nibbling of her ears.

I tore my eyes away and looked up as we took the final step, just in time to see a different head of dark hair. Heather's hair was as rich and glossy as money could buy. Yet it dulled in comparison to Aria's.

Heather's smile tightened. "Brody."

"Heather." I nodded. "Congratulations."

"Thank you." Her gaze darted to Aria, who pressed deeper, almost indecently, into my side. "I don't believe we've met."

"This is Aria Saint-James," I said, not bothering with a bogus label. Girlfriend. Lover. Date. None were accurate and none mattered.

"Congratulations." Aria smiled at Heather, then at Alastair.

"Brody," Alastair greeted with a smug grin. It probably would have been worse had Aria not been on my arm.

My brother was a vain man. He always had his eyes set on whatever shiny toy I had in hand. Whatever I had, he wanted.

Probably why he'd seduced Heather. I highly doubted this was a love match.

"Congratulations." I reached out to shake his hand.

"We missed you at the ceremony." The asshole knew I hadn't been invited.

"That's my fault," Aria said before I could speak. "Brody is irresistible in a tux. It took me a moment to put

60

myself back to rights and by the time we made it here, well . . . we really tried to make it on time."

The color drained from Heather's face and that grin of Alastair's faltered.

I bit back a laugh. God, Aria was something. Fearless. Bold. Unpredictable. Qualities that usually pissed me the fuck off, but tonight, she was on my side. And she was here to put on one hell of a show.

I'd play along.

Bending, I dipped close to her neck, nuzzling the sensitive skin with my nose as I dragged in a heady breath.

She giggled and swatted me away. "Brody, behave."

"With you? Never." I pulled myself away, something that took more effort than it should have, and I faced my brother again. "We're holding up the line. Again, congrats."

I whisked Aria away, not sparing a backward glance. "That went well, don't you think?"

She hummed as her heel twisted, but I kept my grip firm and she didn't stumble. "Damn heels."

"Don't worry. I won't let you fall."

"You do and you die. Now . . . let's find some champagne."

I raised a hand to signal one of the waiters carrying a tray full of flutes. "Pace yourself. This will be a marathon not a—"

"Broderick."

I cringed at my full name and the voice delivering it.

Christ. Was it too much to ask for just one minute between confrontations? Yes. Grandmother wasn't one to give anyone a break, especially her eldest grandson.

She appeared in a flourish. Her jacquard dress and matching jacket were patterned with silver and pale green. Diamond earrings dripped from her ears. A matching pendant hung from her neck. Her white hair had been swept away from her face and twisted into an elegant knot.

"Grandmother." I let go of Aria to take Grandmother's hands in my own. Then I bent and brushed a kiss to her cheek.

"You missed the ceremony," she scolded, shaking her hands free from my grip.

"Apologies." Of course she didn't know I hadn't been invited. Alastair or Heather would have lied.

She tsked, her green eyes scrutinizing me from head to toe.

In my life, only two people had learned to rattle me with a single look. My grandfather. And my grandmother.

My skin itched and I struggled not to squirm as she stared. Then she whipped that cunning gaze to Aria.

I panicked. I should have warned Aria first. Clara knew about my grandmother, had put up with her for years, but this was all new to Aria.

"Who are you?" Grandmother's words were spoken with deliberate breaks, like there was a harsh period between the spaces.

"I am Aria Saint-James." Aria's tone matched Grandmother's, her enunciation nearly as precise and the tone as haughty.

And here I'd been worried for nothing. The knot in my gut eased. I should have expected Aria to meet attitude with attitude. She was not a woman to shrivel like so many dates had in the past under Grandmother's examination.

"You're not Clara," Grandmother declared.

"No, I'm not."

"Then *who* are you?"

"My date," I answered.

Grandmother frowned. "Your taste continues to worsen. Clara might be your employee, but at least the girl can stand up straight and doesn't need to drape herself all over you in public."

"Oh, Brody. You didn't tell me your grandmother was so charming and kind."

Grandmother harumphed. "And she's rude."

"Rude can't be helped." Aria shrugged. "When we drew straws in the womb, Clara picked the ones for poise and grace. That left me with sass and sarcasm."

"*You* are Clara's twin sister?" Grandmother's gaze moved to me. "Why would you bring her here?"

"Because Clara is sick. Aria volunteered to be my guest."

Aria fixed on a sweet smile. "Clara has been telling me for years about Brody's family. The stories seemed so cliché. I mean . . . certainly rich people couldn't really be that shallow. When she got sick, I figured I could come here and see for myself. Per her usual, my sister was right."

I choked on my own spit. *Oh, fuck.*

Grandmother's eyes widened into saucers. "Brody, you embarrass me by bringing a random stray to your brother's wedding."

Aria flinched at the word *stray*. It was small and thankfully Grandmother didn't notice how her word choice had hit a nerve.

Aria opened her mouth, probably to deliver another snarky retort, but I spoke first.

"Then I suppose we'll just be leaving." Maybe this evening would end much, much sooner than I'd planned. No disappointment here.

"You cannot leave." Grandmother frowned. "You know how that would look. Keep her quiet and well away from me. Tonight is not the night for an unseemly display."

"We're not sitting at the same table? Bummer." Aria's voice dripped that fake sugar I'd heard so many times.

For the first time, it tasted delicious.

Grandmother's eyes narrowed and I knew we'd be discussing this on Monday. Then without another word, she disappeared to mingle with her cronies. Namely, Heather's grandmother. Those two were the best of friends and had been for years. I think my broken engagement would have been upsetting if Heather hadn't traded one Carmichael male for the other.

"She's lovely," Aria deadpanned when Grandmother was out of earshot. "Thanks for jumping in there and coming to my rescue."

"You didn't need rescuing."

"True. Is your entire family that kind?"

"That is my entire family. You've met them all." Yes, I had some distant cousins and aunts and uncles, but I'd stopped communicating with them ages ago. When one of them contacted me, it was only for a loan they wouldn't repay. Why bother?

"It's only your brother and grandmother?" Aria asked.

I nodded. "My parents died years ago. In a car accident."

"Oh." The bravado on her face melted away. In its place, a deep sympathy. "I'm sorry."

The murmur of voices filled the ballroom as more people filed inside.

I took Aria's arm and guided her toward a hallway. "Come on."

"Where are we going?" She skipped to keep pace.

"This is where we'll have cocktails. Then we'll be shuffled into another space for dinner. And probably a third for cake and dancing."

"Okay," she drawled. "You didn't answer my question."

No, I didn't. She'd see soon enough.

The guests paid us no attention as we disappeared

from view and slipped into the adjacent room. It was twice as grand as the space where we'd been.

A sea of tables covered in china and silver and enormous floral centerpieces filled the room. Golden lights hung from the ceiling. Archways of more flowers hugged the walls. Their perfume clung thick to the air as we weaved past chairs and empty tables.

I marched us straight for the front, to the row of tables closest to the head table.

It only took me one guess to find my tented place card. I picked it up, along with the one etched for my *guest*. "Be right back."

Aria leaned in to inspect the centerpiece, a tall bouquet of blooms that speared from a gold-dipped vase, while I jogged to the far end of the room and located the table closest to the exit. I searched for two place cards with the same last name. Finding them, I swapped them for my own, then rejoined Aria.

"What did you do?" she asked as I put the tented cards beside Grandmother's.

"Mr. and Mrs. Johnson just got a table upgrade." I held out my elbow for Aria's arm. "Come on."

"You're not worried they'll switch us right back?"

"And make a scene? Never." The wedding planner might be reprimanded for the blunder, but I suspected Alastair would know that I was responsible for the swap.

"You chose the table closest to the bar." Aria smiled as

we walked past our new seating assignments. "Excellent choice."

"Thought you'd approve."

We slipped into the hallway, our steps unhurried as we meandered back to the cocktail room.

There were more people now, more waiters milling about with trays of food. I caught one with a tray of champagne and lifted two flutes, handing one to Aria as we settled next to a table conveniently close to the wall. Like the other tables, it held a floral bouquet.

"These are gorgeous." Aria touched the tip of a white rose. "This visit wasn't entirely wasted. I do love the floral arrangements."

She leaned in, drawing the flower's scent into her nose. Her eyes closed as she inhaled. Savored. The smoky shadow on her eyelids and the dark moons of her lashes were a beautiful sight. Different than her normal makeup-free look.

I stepped closer, close enough that anyone watching would think I was wooing my date. Really, I wanted to talk without prying ears, and if we looked like we were engaged in an intimate conversation, maybe people would leave us alone.

There were enough colleagues and acquaintances here, it wouldn't be long until I was inundated with business conversation. Before that happened, I wanted a quiet moment with Aria.

To apologize.

"And I'm sorry about my grandmother's comment."

"Which one?" she asked, moving away from the bouquet to sip her champagne.

"When she called you a stray."

"Oh." Aria's gaze dropped to the floor. "Does she know? How Clara and I grew up?"

"No, not to my knowledge."

"Then she was just lucky with her shot."

"Still, I apologize on her behalf."

"Don't. She doesn't deserve your grace."

Maybe that was true. But Aria hadn't deserved Grandmother's disdain.

"This is good." Aria raised her glass. "Keep 'em coming, Carmichael."

I chuckled, drinking from my own flute. Aria was right. This event wouldn't be a total bust. And having Aria in Clara's place had already been entertaining.

Clara wouldn't have given Grandmother grief. Clara wouldn't have looked this beautiful in the green dress. Clara wouldn't have pulled me in, closer and closer, until we touched.

Clara might have drawn plenty of eyes from the guests and other men in the room, but she wouldn't have drawn mine.

Clara wasn't Aria.

And Aria had my attention.

"How much do you know about my childhood?" she asked.

"Not much. Enough." Clara and Aria's parents had died in a car accident when they'd been only ten. A drunk driver had crossed the center line and smashed into their car, killing their parents on impact. Afterward, the sisters had gone to live with their uncle. "Clara told me that after you ran away from your uncle, you lived in a junkyard with four other kids."

"That about covers it."

"She said you lived in a van. A delivery van."

A faint smile whispered across Aria's lips. "The other kids, our friends, had their own places. Katherine and Gemma lived in a tent sort of thing, though it was more like a fort. Karson and Londyn lived in the Cadillac that I drove to Arizona. Obviously, it's been restored."

"How did you end up with it?"

"It's on its way across the country, starting in Boston. Clara is going to drive it to California."

"She is? When?"

Aria laughed. "I don't think she's planned it yet. Don't worry. I'm sure she'll plan her trip to coincide with your calendar and clear it first."

"If you actually think she'd ask me, then you don't know who's really in charge. Your sister is the boss. And if you tell her I said that, I'll deny it to the grave."

"My lips are sealed." She smiled, drawing a line across those lips. She hadn't gone for a dark lipstick. They were a natural rose, shiny with gloss.

Her tongue darted out to lick her bottom lip before she took another pull from her flute.

My mouth went dry. My focus was glued to the long, lickable column of her throat as she swallowed.

Back away. Join the crowd. Survive tonight and forget Aria Saint-James.

That was what I should have done.

Yet when she looked up at me, with those beautiful eyes and tempting lips, every reasonable thought went out the window.

"What would you say to stealing a tray of champagne and getting very, very drunk?" I asked.

Aria smiled. "I'd say you were reading my mind."

CHAPTER FIVE

ARIA

"I cannot believe you stole those flowers."

I giggled and set the vase on Brody's kitchen counter, then touched the tip of a calla lily. "Look how beautiful they are. And they smell so good. I couldn't leave them behind to be tossed out."

"They'll die," Brody said.

"Eventually. But not tonight."

First, they'd brighten Brody's concrete home.

I'd been obsessed with the flowers at the reception. Whenever the party had shifted to a new ballroom, the centerpieces had changed to match the space. I'd dragged Brody from vase to vase so I could inspect the arrangements, smell their sweet perfumes and touch their silky petals.

On the way out, the temptation to swipe one had been too much. We'd been alone in the hallway and an elegant vase on one of the tables had called my name. So I'd carried it out the door.

Brody might tease, but I could have sworn I'd heard his kitchen whisper *thank you.*

The room was dim. When we'd come inside, Brody had only flipped on the blue-white lights beneath the cabinets. But it was enough to see that the inside of Brody's home matched the outside. Cold. Drab. Hard. Everything here was a shade of white or gray or black.

The cabinets were a modern style with sleek silver pulls. The floors were wood but the planks had been bleached so the grains and striations were muted. The windows were so clean that the black night seeped through their panes.

The only warmth came from my flowers, my green dress and Brody himself.

In my champagne haze, I studied him with a smile as he walked to the fridge. His polished shoes clicked on the floor and the stainless-steel door opened with a puff.

"We're in luck." He pulled out a bottle of champagne. The glass was a green so dark it was nearly black. The gold foil label screamed *expensive.* Not that I was a champagne connoisseur.

Though I suspected I'd consumed my annual salary's worth of bubbly tonight. The wedding had been an eye-opening study of extravagance. Not even the fanciest of weddings I'd seen at The Gallaway could compare.

The ballrooms alone had wowed. The flowers I'd

taken were likely a thousand-dollar arrangement. It wasn't the season for peonies and tulips. And Juliet roses were pricey no matter the time of year.

There'd been hundreds. Thousands. The plates at dinner, all six varying sizes, had been trimmed in gold. Every glass had been crystal. The food itself had been delish, course after course, every bite decadent.

And the champagne had flowed in rivers. The servers, dressed in crisp white shirts and sharp black vests, had never let my flute go dry.

A dream wedding.

I was still dreaming. Because only in sleep could Brody be so . . . fun.

We'd laughed and talked and ignored the other guests at our table. He'd told me stories about people at the wedding. He'd entertained me with tales of blind dates with a few women in attendance. He'd laughed along as I'd impersonated his stuffy grandmother. And together, we'd heckled and teased every one of the toast makers. Twenty-eight in total. Why someone needed to have twenty-eight toasts at their wedding I would never comprehend.

Brody and I had been that couple, the annoying one who'd had fun despite being miserable, and yes, it had been at the expense of some others. I'd never see those people again and couldn't find the motivation to feel guilty.

The champagne bottle hissed before the cork loosened

with a pop. It flew across the room and bounced off a wall. A spray of foam splattered the floor.

"Whoops." Brody ignored it and walked to a cabinet, opening it to pull out two flutes. They clinked on the silver-veined white granite counters. The champagne fizzed as he filled the glasses to nearly overflowing.

He handed me one, then lifted his own. "Cheers."

"Cheers." My cheeks pinched from so much smiling.

My head was fuzzy and tomorrow I'd have a bitch of a hangover. I drained my flute regardless. More alcohol wasn't the responsible choice, except it was delicious and I wasn't ready to go home yet.

Clara and August were asleep. By all rights, I should be dead on my bare feet—my shoes had lasted until the flight home, then I'd kicked them off and left them forgotten on the plane. Maybe Ron, the bowing butler, had picked them up when he'd collected us from the Welcome airport in a town car and driven us home.

It was two o'clock in the morning, well past my normal bedtime, but my body pulsed with restless energy. It was adrenaline from the party. A buzz from the champagne. And a high from Brody.

His aura was invigorating, his grin charming. His quick wit and dry sense of humor had kept a smile on my face all night. The brooding, grumpy billionaire would likely surface tomorrow, but tonight, I was enjoying this version of Brody. The version with a personality.

Maybe this was why Clara had worked for him after

these many years. Maybe when Brody let his guard down, he was actually . . . nice.

"Thank you, Aria." He set his glass down and hopped up to sit on the edge of the massive island.

"You're welcome." I set my own flute on the counter at my back, planting my hands on the edge and hopping up too. The gown's skirt swished over my toes, the satin cool and smooth against my skin.

"Tonight was . . . unexpected." The rich baritone of his rugged voice warmed the lifeless room. It was as intoxicating as the champagne. More than once tonight, I'd let him lean in close and whisper in my ear.

More than once, I'd pretended the flirts were real. "Quite unexpected. And fun. Do you ever have fun?"

He chuckled and a shiver rolled down my spine. "Not often. I certainly hadn't planned on fun tonight."

"Does it bother you? Heather and Alastair?" I'd wanted to ask all night but had restrained myself until now. Did he still love her?

"Yes," he admitted. "But not for the reason you think. I don't like that Alastair won."

"Ah. Then it's a competition."

"Between us, yes." He lifted his glass to those soft lips for another sip. "We're not like you and Clara. We never have been. He's five years younger than I am, and I swear we've been battling since the day he was born."

Clara was my best friend. My confidant. My sister of

blood and soul. Warring with a sibling seemed unnecessarily sad. "I'm sorry."

He shrugged, then he lifted a hand to touch the bouquet. "These are wasted on me. You should take them to Clara."

"No. Leave them here. This place is in desperate need of color." Even though the flowers were all pale shades of pink and peach and cream, at least they were warm.

"You don't like my house?"

"Not especially."

A grin spread across his handsome face. "What would you change?"

"Oh . . . everything. But mostly, I'd add some life. Color. Texture. You do know they make paint in actual shades besides greige, right?"

"Do they?" he teased. "I'll be sure to tell my interior designer. I bet your home is full of life."

"You'd hate it. There are colors everywhere. And plants. Lots and lots of plants."

He chuckled again, draining the rest of his glass. "Do you like your job?"

"I love my job. I like working with my hands and seeing things grow under my care. It's satisfying, seeing a flower blossom and knowing I'm the one who planted the seed."

"How did it start? How did you become interested in gardening?" He leaned forward, his gaze fixed on me. Brody had been like that all night. When I spoke, he listened. Intently. It had been unnerving at first. Now, I couldn't seem to stop myself from talking because his attention was addictive.

"It started at the junkyard. It was so . . . dead."

"Like my home."

I laughed. "Yes, but in a different shade. Dirt and rust. Everything had this reddish-orange tinge. I don't know why I got the impulse, but I was at the grocery store one day buying a loaf of bread, and beside the checkout stand, they had this display of packets. You know, the metal stand with all the seeds?"

He shook his head. "No, but I believe you."

"Have you ever been inside a grocery store?"

"Once or twice."

I shook my head and laughed. "God, our lives are different. Anyway, the packets were only thirty cents, so I bought three of them. I wanted to do something to make my little world prettier. I planted the seeds in an old egg carton and prayed they'd grow."

"You gave it life."

"I tried." I gave him a sad smile. "It was a hobby. Tending my plants and flowers gave me something to do. By the time I left, Lou had enough to start a greenhouse if he wanted."

"Lou?"

"The owner of the junkyard," I said. "He let us stay there."

"Right. The recluse. Clara never told me his name."

77

"Lou Miley. I think I only spoke to him once or twice during the years we were there. He let us be. We did the same for him. But there was a fondness there, even from a distance."

When Clara and I had left the junkyard, I'd replanted everything I'd grown and staged it closer to his home. I'd never forget the look on Lou's face when he spotted the pink flowers I'd left right outside his door. He gaped at them, shocked, and maybe a little bit proud.

I liked to think that he'd watered those flowers after I'd left. That he'd realized it had been the only thing I could give him as a token of my appreciation.

I'd given him the lives I'd grown as thanks for saving mine.

"Enough about that." I waved the topic away. I didn't think about the junkyard often or, even more rarely, the miserable years before. And tonight, I was enjoying myself too much to rehash the past.

Besides, it wasn't like Brody actually cared. I suspected this charm was his way of humoring me. His own token of appreciation for accompanying him tonight.

"You work at a hotel," he said.

"I do." I nodded. "The Gallaway. It's beautiful. Different than the hotel we were at tonight, but no less exquisite. It's right on the coast. I get to work with the ocean waves as my soundtrack and the smell of salt and sand in the air."

"You love your home. You love your job. What else should I know about you, Aria Saint-James?"

That maybe I don't hate you. "One day, I'd like to have a flower shop and a greenhouse of my own. I'd like to make bouquets like that one and keep growing plants."

It was a secret I hadn't told anyone, not even Clara. I didn't set many goals. I didn't think too far into the future. Because it was too easy for dreams to be stolen. Better they stay locked away.

"I don't know why I just told you that," I admitted.

"Probably the champagne."

I lifted my glass for another sip. "Probably. And tomorrow, I'll regret confiding in the enemy."

"I'm still the enemy?" he asked.

"Of course."

"Good." He grinned, hopping off the counter. "Come tomorrow, there will be no more need for a truce."

"Agreed." The word sounded breathy as he crossed the space between us.

There was hunger in his green eyes. It had been there for hours. If he pulled a mirror from his tux pocket, I'd likely see that same desire in my own gaze. He walked closer, his gait easy and confident. Each step was a seduction, like the one and only dance we'd shared at the wedding.

Brody had held me tight, his grip on my waist firm. And he'd given me that attention, that undivided attention. The spice of his cologne filled my nose as he closed the gap. With me seated on the counter, our eyes were nearly level. Not quite. He stood a few inches over six feet, and even with my perch, he had me beat.

His beard seemed thicker in the muted light and my fingers itched to touch the strands. His hair was combed so well, it needed a good tousle.

"What are you doing?" I asked as he inched closer, pressing into the skirt of my gown.

"I'm going to kiss you."

My heart skipped. *Yes*. That was the champagne talking. I didn't care. "What if I don't want you to kiss me?"

He leaned in close, the warmth of his breath caressing my cheek. "What if you do?"

What if I did?

I took his face in my hands, letting the scratch of his beard scrape against my palms, and I pulled his mouth down to mine.

Then *I* kissed *him*.

———

"HEY," Clara said, walking into the living room.

"Shhhh." I held up a finger from my spot on the couch. "Not so loud."

"Headache?"

I groaned. "I'll never drink champagne again."

She laughed and plopped down by my feet, taking my

legs and pulling them over her lap. Then she massaged the arch of a foot. "How was it?"

"Fine." I closed my eyes and did my best to block out the image of last night. Not of the wedding.

Of Brody's bed.

God, what the hell had I been thinking? Why? Why had I slept with him? Sex with Clara's boss was the worst decision I'd made in years. Worse than the time I'd cut my own bangs seven years ago.

Brody was . . . irresistible. Damn him for being so. I didn't even like him. Did I?

He'd been out cold this morning when I'd woken up early. It was the lifelong habit of a groundskeeper to rise before dawn and prune and water before hotel guests made their way outside and tripped over my hoses.

So as he'd slumbered, I'd silently slipped out of his bed and into my dress, then raced from his bedroom. I'd hoped to save myself from the walk of shame, but butler Ron had been in the kitchen, washing last night's champagne flutes.

He'd given me another goddamn bow just before I'd made it to the door. Then I'd hustled to Clara's, hoping not to wake her or Gus as I'd showered, dressed in sweats and crashed here on the couch.

"Thank you for going," Clara said, her foot massage saving my life.

"Sure. How are you feeling?"

"Better."

"Good." I closed my eyes. Bad idea. The image of

Brody's naked body—muscled arms, washboard abs, impressive arousal—popped into my mind.

I groaned. *Such. An. Idiot.* This was his fault. Why did he have to have such an amazing body? Why was he so handsome? Why did he have to be such a good kisser?

That first kiss had been my downfall. His tongue had slid between my teeth and goodbye common sense.

My body ached, not just from the hangover, but from being used. Incredibly, sinfully used. Brody Carmichael knew how to give a woman an orgasm. With his fingers. With his tongue. With his thick, long, talented—

I groaned again. *Curse you, Brody.* It would have been so much easier to keep hating him if he hadn't been so... perfect.

"Are you getting sick?" Clara asked. "Oh, no. I hope you don't have what I had."

"I'm sure it's just the hangover." The sex hangover.

"Tell me about the wedding."

"It was beautiful. Expensive. They spent more money on a party than I've made in three years. Or more."

"Strange, aren't they?" Clara asked. "Rich people."

"Strange what they think is important."

"Brody gets it," she said. "Even though he has more money than is healthy, he gets it."

Yesterday, I would have argued. Yesterday, I would have told her that when it came to her boss, she was delusional. But yesterday, I hadn't known Brody.

Or maybe that was just wishful thinking on my part.

Maybe that was me wanting to believe that I hadn't let a rich jerk seduce me into a one-night stand.

I hated the idea that it all might have been a game. That he'd used me for sex. That I'd fallen for a trick.

"You aren't arguing with me," Clara said. "That means you really are hungover."

I forced a smile. "Do my other foot. And stop talking so loud."

She giggled and continued my massage.

We sat there, in comfortable companionship and quiet, until Gus woke up and, headache or not, I roused from the couch to spend time with my family.

We were outside on the front lawn when I heard a door close.

I looked down the driveway just in time to see Brody carry a duffel bag to his Jag.

He was wearing sunglasses. A suit, per usual. He looked striking and every bit a polished billionaire. The champagne didn't seem to have paled his skin like it had mine.

Brody got into his car and drove away without a word. Without a glance.

And two weeks later, when I returned home to Oregon, I reminded myself that Brody Carmichael was an asshole. My pride had kept me from asking Clara where he'd gone. It had also kept me from telling her that I'd fucked her boss.

Brody was the enemy. He was a one-night mistake and a man I didn't have to see again if I was lucky.

It didn't matter that he'd left Arizona, escaping my company. It didn't matter that I'd been just another willing body in his bedroom. It didn't matter that I'd fallen for him, just a little.

That night didn't matter.

And I'd forget about it soon enough anyway.

CHAPTER SIX

ARIA

I *hate Brody Carmichael.*

"Oh, God." I slid to my butt on the bathroom floor, letting the cold from the tile seep into my jeans. My stomach churned and I rose up just in time to retch into the toilet. Again.

How much puking could a woman do when she hadn't eaten anything in twelve hours?

Apparently, a lot. This was the fourth time I'd had to rush to the bathroom this morning.

I wiped my mouth dry and waited, hovering beside the porcelain to make sure I was done. Then I glanced at my watch. Eleven o'clock. That was usually when the vomiting stopped.

Why? Why had I been so foolish? Why had I had so much champagne? Why had I let Clara talk me into going to that wedding two months ago?

And why had I slept with Brody?

That son of a bitch Carmichael got me pregnant.

Pregnant.

That word had been bouncing around in my brain for two days, ever since I'd held the positive test in my hand. *Pregnant.* Only reading the result a thousand times had helped it sink in.

When I'd missed my period, I'd fooled myself into thinking it was an anomaly. I'd chalked it up to exercise. After my trip to Arizona, I'd started working out hard at the gym in Heron Beach. They'd started a pre-holiday workout challenge, and after jumping and squatting and crunching, most nights I'd walked home like a limp noodle.

The class was a killer, but I had more muscle definition at thirty than I'd had at twenty. Women lost their periods from body fat changes all the time, right?

Denial was an evil bitch. She'd trick you into false securities. She'd duped me into ignoring the real reason I hadn't bought my monthly supply of tampons. Then, after weeks of being my constant companion, she'd abandoned me.

My exhaustion hadn't faded, even after cutting time at the gym. My breasts were tender. My mind sluggish. And my stomach in a constant knot.

One week of morning sickness and the signs were all there, screaming at me to stop ignoring the truth.

Pregnant. I was going to become a mother.

And I had no idea what to do.

When Clara had realized she was pregnant with August, she'd called me crying from the bathroom in her Las Vegas apartment. She'd been hysterical. Her sobs had bounced off the walls.

What am I going to do? What am I going to do?

She'd asked me that question over and over. Once she'd calmed down, we'd spent hours talking it through. Her biggest fear had been telling Devan. Maybe because she'd known how he'd react.

Though handsome, Devan hadn't been the most loving of boyfriends. He was a narcissist. A child, even his own, would be competition for attention. There were times when he worshiped Clara, enough to make her stay. But a baby? Clara knew he was going to flip that her birth control hadn't worked. He proved predictable.

After breaking the news, she called me again, from the same bathroom, this time livid because Devan had accused her of doing it on purpose.

Would Brody do the same?

From what I could remember, he'd used condoms. Multiple condoms. One of them must have broken. And since I wasn't one to bring men to my bed, or sleep in theirs, I hadn't bothered with birth control. Sex for me was as rare as the steak tartare served at the wedding reception.

Stupid, Aria. Don't think about food.

My stomach rolled again, but being empty, nothing

came up. That would change tomorrow morning when I'd repeat this blessed cycle again.

I shoved myself off the floor and out of the bathroom stall, then went to the sink to splash water on my face. The bottle of mouthwash in my purse was nearly empty but I had enough for a swish and spit.

When I chanced a look at my reflection, the mirror showed me that I looked the way I felt. Like shit.

My face was pale. The purple circles under my eyes were darker than they'd been yesterday. My shoulders slumped because the weight on them was so heavy I couldn't muster the strength to snap them straight.

Pregnancy had more of a greenish tinge than a glow.

What am I going to do?

Was I ready for this? I'd hoped kids would come after I'd found the man of my dreams. How was I going to do this on my own?

One day at a time. That's what I'd told Clara when she'd been the woman in the bathroom. I'd heed my own advice.

First things first, it was time to tell my sister. Two days, and this secret was barking to be let out of its cage. Clara had done this before. She'd navigated a pregnancy and faced single motherhood. Clara would make it all better— after she reamed my ass for sleeping with her boss.

"I'm going to tell her." I nodded to myself. "Today. As soon as I feel better."

Before my reflection could convince me one more day

of secrecy wouldn't hurt, I walked away from the sink. The women's locker room at The Gallaway was empty. Most of the staff had already dropped off their personal belongings to start work for the day.

This time of year, the hotel wasn't as busy as it was during the warmer months. December's pace around the hotel was slower as the guest count dwindled. The housekeepers were less frantic. The grounds staff had been cut down to the bare minimum. Our seasonal workers would return in the spring.

With Christmas only five days away, this week would be one of the quietest all year. Though some families came to celebrate at The Gallaway, per their annual tradition. They'd be fussed over and given extra attention. Our chef was busy preparing for extravagant holiday meals.

Any other year and the kitchen would have been a regular stop on my daily rounds. But now, with the smells and my queasy stomach, I'd been avoiding that end of the hotel for the same reason I avoided marigolds in planters. They stank.

I wandered down the hallway, fighting to put on a happy face. I was five minutes late for a meeting with my boss, Andy, the new general manager.

Mark had hired Andy earlier this year, and the duties I'd covered as temporary GM had been handed over, but Andy insisted we continue this daily meeting. *I'm too tired for this.*

Regardless, I made my way to the lobby. Three

Christmas trees decorated the vast space, each with golden lights and silver ribbons that had been wrapped in perfect spirals around the boughs. The crystal chandelier hanging low in the center of the space cast fractured beams across the marble floors.

The hotel looked magical, though I still preferred the spring and summer, when fresh flowers decorated the space and my plants greeted guests as they strolled through the wide front entrance.

I waved at the receptionist stationed at the desk, then disappeared through the door behind the counter marked for employees only. Then, using the last of my reserves, I trudged up the staircase to the second floor.

The corner office, Mark's, was dark. In the winter, he took Wednesdays off as personal days. His beachfront home was as impressive as his hotel, and if I owned it, I'd make it a point to spend time there too.

Beside Mark's was Andy's office. It wasn't quite as impressive as the corner, but with the view overlooking the ocean and the cliffs that gave way to the sandy beach, it sure didn't suck.

Forcing some pep into my expression, I knocked on Andy's door.

"Come in."

I turned the knob and entered. "Hey."

"Aria." He stood from his desk and straightened the lapel on his suit jacket. Then he smiled, a pleasant smile but one that betrayed his feelings.

Andy's crush on me was the worst-kept secret at The Gallaway.

"Please, allow me." He rounded his desk and pulled out the guest chair. "Have a seat."

"Thanks." I shied away as he lingered just a second too long beside the armrest.

Awkward and uncomfortable crush aside, Andy had proved to be a good boss in the months he'd been here. He treated the staff with kindness. He worked hard and had earned Mark's respect. But Andy was a single man in his midforties, and the affection he had for me was as obvious as the waves crashing onto the shore outside.

"Have you had lunch?" he asked, returning to his side of the desk.

Beyond him and through the windows, the winter sky was a lighter shade of gray than the ocean itself. Part of me wanted to find a quiet bench somewhere on the sprawling deck outside, curl up under a blanket and let the caw of the seagulls lull me to sleep.

How was I going to manage my job and a baby? It was possible. Deep down, I knew I'd figure it out, but the logistics escaped me at the moment. The idea of searching for daycare and babysitters was overwhelming. Today, this week, the future looked as hazy as the horizon outside where the sea met the clouds.

"Aria?"

"Huh?" I blinked, tearing my gaze away from the glass to focus on Andy's face. "Sorry. No, I haven't had lunch."

"Should I order something for us?" He gestured to the desk phone. "I heard the chef made a large pot of clam chowder today and it's delicious."

I gagged. "No. No lunch for me today."

"Oh." His face fell, but he recovered quickly with a smile. His blond hair was combed smartly at a part over his left eyebrow. His face was always clean shaven. Maybe in another life, Andy would have been a nice man to date.

I suspected he enjoyed long walks on the beach and romantic candlelit dinners. We'd never bicker or fight. Andy was much too polite for sarcasm.

Dating would soon become a distant memory, not that I'd dated much these past few years. Even Andy wouldn't want to get involved with a pregnant woman. Baggage might as well be my middle name.

"Sorry," I said. "It's not you. I'm just not feeling great today."

"Is there anything I can do?" The concern on his face was endearing. As a friend.

"I'll be fine." The new mantra. I'd be fine. *We'd* be fine. I fought the urge to press a hand to my belly. "My plan is to spend a few hours in the greenhouse. That always perks me up."

"Then don't let me keep you." He stood from his chair. "We can skip today's meeting. Catch up later."

"Are you sure?"

"Of course." He came to my chair, pulling it out for

me as I stood. "We'll talk when you get back from Arizona."

Tomorrow, I was leaving to spend Christmas with Clara and August. My suitcase was packed and my flight booked.

Never in my life had I dreaded a trip to see my family.

"Merry Christmas and Happy New Year, Andy."

"Same to you, Aria."

I waved, then headed for the door. I didn't linger at the hotel. The fresh air outside beckoned, so I collected my jacket from the locker room and ducked out the employee exit. My condo wasn't far from the hotel, only blocks, and rather than drive, I walked to work most days.

Now that I'd left the Cadillac with Clara, I didn't have a vehicle. Not long before Katherine had come to Oregon with the Cadillac, I'd sold my old Jetta. It had been a piece of junk and prone to breakdowns and flat tires. I'd been searching for a replacement but then the Cadillac had magically appeared and voila. No more car shopping.

Besides, Heron Beach was a small town. Walking the streets was safe and the grocery store delivered.

The air wrapped around me cool and sharp, chasing the last dregs of nausea away. The Gallaway had golf carts for my staff to use for going back and forth between the off-site greenhouse and storage area five blocks away, but I hadn't climbed behind the wheel of one in ages.

Much like my journey to and from home, I preferred to hoof it.

The walk was invigorating, and by the time I made it to the greenhouse, my spirits had lifted. The future didn't seem quite as bleak. And though Clara was going to be surprised, maybe there'd be a little excitement there too.

I was having a baby.

My baby.

There'd never be a day when I was alone. There'd never be a day when I longed for a family. I was growing one. The life inside me deserved my best. He or she would have it. From now until my dying breath.

It was . . . exciting. Scary, but wonderful.

Digging the keys from my coat pocket, I unlocked the greenhouse door and stepped inside. Dirt and leaves and water. I breathed it all in, holding the air in my lungs for a moment.

"Better." I sighed, shrugging off my coat.

The greenhouse was my favorite place. A sanctuary. Here, we created life. We made messes. My staff all knew that when you were at The Gallaway, you smiled at guests but stayed in the periphery. The greenhouse was where we could all let loose and be ourselves.

Here, the world made sense. Here, I could figure this pregnancy thing out.

I meandered down the aisles between planting tables, my tennis shoes crunching on the gravel floor. There were a few poinsettias left that hadn't been perfect enough for the hotel. This morning, I'd earmarked each for my employees to take home. The seedling trays were mostly stacked and empty. We wouldn't fill and plant the majority of them until February or March, depending on the varietal. But the scent from the plants lingered year-round.

The small desk at the far end of the greenhouse was cluttered with papers. My laptop was collecting dust. Two forgotten water bottles joined the mess. The space served as my office, where I'd place supply orders and draft work schedules and answer the rare email.

When I'd worked as the temporary GM, I'd used Andy's office. The view was spectacular but spending my time there had been beautiful torture. I wasn't meant for a fancy office and paperwork. Though I'd muddled through fine, making sure that everyone had their duties covered, it had never fit. Not like the greenhouse. This was where I was most comfortable. This was where I was the most productive. This was where life made sense.

Most days.

I plopped into my black upholstered chair, spinning it to the desk and slouching down deep. Then I dug my phone from my pocket to make the call—or calls—that were two days overdue.

Clara answered on the second ring. "Hey. All set for tomorrow?"

"Yep." I sucked in a deep breath. I couldn't fly to Arizona and spend the day with her and August, waiting for him to go to bed, with this news hanging over my head. She'd know from the moment she picked me up at the airport that something was wrong. And this was not news I wanted to deliver with August in the car. "Got a second? I need to tell you something."

"I don't like that tone," she said. "What's wrong?"

I gulped. "I'm pregnant."

"W-what?"

"I'm pregnant."

"Oh." The silence dragged after that one pained syllable. "I, um . . . I didn't realize you were seeing someone."

"I'm not." God, this was hard. And about to get worse. "It was a one-time thing."

"Are you okay?"

"No," I admitted, tears welling in my eyes. "But I will be."

Tomorrow, when I could soak up one of her hugs, I'd tell her I was scared. I'd tell her I didn't know how to be a mother, not after we'd lost our own so young. I'd tell her that I didn't know how to fit an infant into my life, and I had no idea how to incorporate Brody into the mix.

"What can I do?" Clara asked.

My heart squeezed. "I'll be ready for a hug tomorrow."

"I'll have one waiting."

"And I need . . ." I closed my eyes. Damn it, this sucked.

"You need what?"

I swallowed down my fears and braced. "I need Brody's number."

"Why—" She gasped, putting the pieces together. "He's the father?"

I nodded.

"Aria?"

"Yes," I whispered. "It happened after the wedding."

"Um . . ." She trailed off and stayed quiet. Then she cleared her throat. "He's right here. Let me give him the phone."

"Wait. Clara—" Too late.

She'd taken the phone from her ear before I could tell her that I wasn't ready to talk to Brody yet. I wanted his number so I could call him before my flight tomorrow, but I hadn't worked out what to say yet.

Clara's voice echoed in the background as she spoke to Brody. "Phone call for you."

"Who is it?" His deep voice hit my ear and my panic spiked.

Tell him.

I was going to puke again. I'd survived plenty of hard moments in my life. The death of my parents. Living with my uncle. Running away at fifteen. But for some reason, this seemed like the hardest of them all.

My entire body trembled as I listened, waiting for Brody to get on the line.

Clara said my name, then there was a long pause.

"What?"

One word and all my fears disappeared. One bark

from an arrogant jerk and I wasn't scared anymore. No, I was pissed. "Hello to you too."

"I'm busy, Aria."

"God, you are an asshole. I hope our baby gets his or her personality from me."

"W-what?"

So he wasn't a complete robot. I'd rattled him. *Good.* I was rattled too. "You heard me."

Brody went still. The air in the greenhouse swirled from the fans that we ran year-round. Their hum was the only noise. Not even his breath registered in my ear.

"Brody," I said.

No response, not even to ask me if I was sure he was the father.

"Brody."

Dead air.

I pulled the phone away from my ear and my mouth fell open. It was quiet because he'd hung up on me. "That son of a bitch."

Tossing the phone to the table, I shot out of my chair and stalked through the greenhouse. He'd hung up on me. He'd actually hung up on me. My fingers itched to strangle something—or someone, but that someone lived in Arizona.

"How dare he hang up on me? How fucking dare he?" My voice bounced around the empty room. "Grrr. I hate him."

I walked the length of the greenhouse twice, my anger

growing with each step. Sitting at my desk would only make me crazy, so I grabbed a pair of leather gloves and got to work. I pulled a stool up to a table and began planting some seeds for the spring greenery. Million bells. Cosmos. Zinnias. It wasn't on the schedule to start them until January, but a few extra days wouldn't hurt.

I'd never been fancy with the varieties we planted. My predecessor and mentor hadn't been either. He'd taught me that sometimes the most amazing displays were nothing more than abundant color. I preferred hardy plants that would survive the regular touches from guests and the sniffs from pets and kids.

My anger at Brody kept me company while I lost myself in the dirt and seeds and quiet whirl of the green-house. Clara tried to call a few times but I pushed her to voicemail and sent her a text that I'd call later. I couldn't talk to her, not when she was so close to Brody. *Bastard.*

Hours later, well past the noon hour and close to dinner, my stomach growled so loudly the sound echoed in the greenhouse.

An enormous appetite came crashing down, and for the first time today, I was ravenous. The same had happened yesterday and the day before. My body didn't want a thing before four, then afterward, I'd eat and eat and eat until bedtime.

Quickly tidying up my workspace, I returned to my desk for my coat and keys. I jotted down a message on a sticky note for the staff to water the seed trays I'd planted while I was in Arizona for the holiday, though the note was unnecessary.

The winter grounds crew was the full-time crew. They were all at the hotel, completing the short to-do list I'd assigned this morning. If there was a snow flurry, they'd take care of the shoveling and plowing. They'd ice the sidewalks. And they'd water, inside the hotel and here too.

Today wasn't the first time I'd been in a mood that had resulted in new plants to tend.

With the greenhouse locked, I rushed along the sidewalk to The Gallaway, hoping the chef had something warm. The clam chowder would do. Or pasta. Or chowder *and* pasta. Maybe some bread too.

Could I eat clam chowder? I typed in a quick search on my phone. Soon, I'd have to find a doctor and learn the specifics. Clara had cut out certain things when she'd been pregnant with August, but since we hadn't lived together, I couldn't remember the exact items.

Today, all I cared about was that clam chowder was safe and so were carbs.

In the kitchen, the chef greeted me with a wide smile, as though he'd expected to see me. After only days, my odd eating schedule was becoming predictable. He whipped up a bowl of chowder and one of his fancy grilled cheese sandwiches. I devoured it all in the employee break room along with a cookie and a Coke from the vending machine.

With a full belly and a subdued temper, I pulled out my phone and called my sister.

"Hey," Clara answered. "You okay?"

"I don't know," I admitted.

"Brody is—"

"Don't. Please," I begged. "I don't want to talk about Brody. Not right now."

"Okay. Do you still want to come here tomorrow?"

"Yes." I wasn't letting Brody steal my Christmas. "I'll be there."

Maybe if I was lucky, he'd find somewhere else to spend the holidays. Yes, we had a lot to discuss and figure out, but it could wait. We had months, if Brody even wanted to be involved.

Would he want to be in our child's life? Or would he be like Devan and disappear? My heart sank. How was I going to explain to a kid that his father didn't want him? That her dad had abandoned her in favor of private jets and cold mansions?

Maybe Brody would surprise me. Maybe he'd stick. How were we going to raise a child from different states? How would we handle holidays? Would I only get to have my baby every other special occasion?

"There's so much to figure out," I whispered.

"You will."

"Yeah," I murmured. "We'll have lots to talk about tomorrow."

"Talking would be good."

"I'm sorry I didn't tell you about Brody."

"I understand." And the truth in her voice eased some of the guilt. We'd figure this out, like we had every hurdle life had put in our path. Together.

"I'll text you when I'm at the airport tomorrow."

"Love you," she said.

I smiled. "I love you too."

The next shift was due to start soon and one of the night-shift clerks came in to leave his dinner in the employee fridge. I waved, talked to him for a moment, then headed out to the lobby.

"Aria." Andy was at the receptionist counter and his entire face brightened when I walked through the door.

I forced a smile. "Hey."

"Feeling better?"

"I am, thanks." Surprisingly, much better. Now that I'd told Clara, I wasn't alone in this. Secrets had never been my thing and sharing the news that I was going to have a baby had lightened the load.

That was how it worked with Clara. We shared burdens.

Pregnancies. Brody.

If he abandoned our baby, at least I wouldn't have to convince Clara to quit and move to Oregon. There was no way she'd stay with him if he turned out to be a deadbeat dad.

"It's cold out." Andy nodded toward the french doors that opened to the deck on the ocean side of the hotel. In the summer, those doors were rarely closed. "I was just taking off for the day. Would you like a ride home?"

He was just so . . . clueless. And nice. Refusing him was not easy. When was he going to realize this was never going to happen?

I opened my mouth, my brain scrambling for a gentle rejection, when a flash of dark caught my eye over Andy's shoulder.

A man in a crisp black suit strode into the hotel, his green gaze locked on my face.

Brody.

CHAPTER SEVEN

BRODY

"What are you doing here?" Aria asked through a clenched jaw.

The guy beside her stepped closer, hovering beside her elbow. He lifted his hand, ready to touch her, but at my glare, he must have thought better of it and let his arm drop to his side.

I dismissed him and focused on the woman.

Aria's face was pale. The circles under her eyes looked more like bruises. And she'd lost weight—weight she hadn't had to lose.

"You look awful."

She crossed her arms over her chest. "You came all the way to Oregon to tell me I look awful."

The man stepped closer to Aria, positioning himself between us.

The look I sent him was the one I'd used countless

times in the conference room. One I'd learned from Grandmother. People withered under the look. This guy did.

The only person who seemed immune was Aria.

Her scowl deepened, then vanished when she turned to him. "Andy, would you excuse me?"

"Is everything okay?" He touched her elbow.

I tensed.

Aria tensed. It was slight but visible. She gave *Andy* a tight smile. "All good. Thank you."

He reluctantly nodded and dropped his hand once more, but did he leave? Andy just stood there, staring at her like she was the sun and the moon and the stars.

Christ. I didn't have time to deal with a boyfriend. Was he her boyfriend? Because I wasn't okay with that. I wasn't okay with another man touching her. Kissing her. Definitely not sleeping with her.

My head, which had been spinning since her phone call earlier, was close to exploding. It was only by sheer force of will that I hadn't had a complete and total mental breakdown—not that I'd ever had a breakdown.

But if there was a time, this was it.

The idea of this guy being in her life. Taking my place. *No. Fuck no.*

I was the father. This was my kid. Maybe. I hoped. Probably.

"Aria," I gritted out. Did she not see me coming out of my skin here?

Another glare for me. Another pained smile for Andy. "Have a merry Christmas."

"You too." Andy backed away and, finally, turned and disappeared down a hallway.

Leaving me and Aria in the middle of a hotel lobby to stare at one another.

She did look awful. Worse than awful.

And beautiful.

I'd had a hard time getting her off my mind since the wedding. For two months, I'd done my best to return to normal life. Work had been busy and I'd used it as an escape. But in the dark hours, when I was at home alone, I'd find myself in the kitchen, wishing those flowers she'd stolen hadn't died.

She'd been right. They had added some life to the house.

Her scent, floral and sweet, had disappeared from my bedroom the morning after she'd left. Ron was too good at his job at times and had washed my sheets while I'd been in the shower. But I could still picture Aria in my bed, sleeping soundly with the slightest smile on her face.

When I closed my eyes, her silky hair greeted me first. Then her eyes. Those molten, chocolate eyes with the fiery flecks. Next came her coy smile. The one she'd flashed me countless times at the wedding.

Aria Saint-James was impossible to escape.

And now she was pregnant. With my baby.

Pregnant.

I'd been playing that word in my head, over and over. Rolling it around. Testing its severity. For three hours during the flight, I'd mentally repeated it on loop. It was so . . . enormous. Eight letters that had changed my life.

The concept was too much. Too big. So I'd deal with a smaller one first.

"Who is that?" I nodded in the direction where Andy had disappeared.

"Andy is my boss."

"He's in love with you."

"No, he isn't." She rolled her eyes. "He has a little crush on me. Nothing more. It's awkward but temporary."

Temporary. Clearly, she didn't realize the depth of Andy's feelings. Or that nothing about her rendered temporary. Aria had a lasting effect. She walked into your life and you struggled to remember what it had been like before you'd seen that first smile.

"Why did you come here, Brody?"

"You're . . ." I gulped.

"Pregnant."

That word was like a bullet racing out the barrel of a gun. By some miracle, my knees didn't buckle. Hearing it from her lips, watching them form the word, there was no denying it. That didn't stop me from asking a dumb question.

"You're sure?"

"Uh, yeah." Another eye roll. "Why would I lie?"

Because it wouldn't be the first time a woman had

tried. But Aria had moral fiber. She wouldn't understand that a child with me meant the payday of a lifetime. "And it's—"

"If you ask me if it's yours, I will cut your balls off and string them on the Christmas tree."

I held up a hand. "That's not what I was going to say."

"Oh."

"It's okay? Healthy? You're okay?"

She dropped her gaze to the shiny marble floor. "I'm tired. I feel like shit. Probably why I look awful, as you so graciously pointed out."

"Sorry." I dragged a hand over my bearded jaw.

"What are you doing here, Brody?" she asked again.

"I'm in a little bit of shock. I had to make sure."

"A phone call would have sufficed. Or you could have not hung up on me in the first place."

Not an option. The moment her announcement had set in, I'd had to see her. In person. I'd had to watch with my own eyes as my ears heard the word come from her lips.

Aria was pregnant. The truth settled into my bones. The world that had been spinning in one direction suddenly shifted, spinning on an entirely different axis. One that was centered around the life growing inside her.

There was a lot of shit to figure out.

"Join me for dinner."

"I just ate."

I checked my watch. "At four o'clock?"

She shrugged. "I eat when I'm hungry. That doesn't happen all the time, so I take advantage."

"Coffee? Decaf. Please."

"What do you want, Brody?" Her frame slumped. Her voice held so much exhaustion, all I wanted was to scoop her up and tuck her into my bed for the rest of the week.

"To talk. I want to talk."

"Okay." She nodded. "I was just on my way home."

"Lead the way."

She gave me the side-eye, then shrugged on her coat. I followed close behind as she walked past me and out the front doors.

I fell into step beside her on the sidewalk, keeping up with her brisk pace. The cold air bit into my ears and nose. Where was her car?

Aria kept walking, following the curve of the street. I expected her to stop at one of the parking lots, but she kept on going.

Then we changed directions after a few blocks, starting up a side street. Step by silent step, we made our way farther and farther from the hotel and the sound of the ocean.

She shouldn't be walking, not when she was this tired. Not at this hour. The sun was beginning to set. In an hour, it would be almost dark. Even now, the light was dim enough to mute the colors of the homes we passed.

The leaves had fallen from the trees, their limbs bare. The grassy lawns looked to have been frozen a time or twelve. It was just . . . cold. The damp chill from the humid air seeped through my suit coat and made me shiver. I clenched my teeth to keep them from chattering.

It was too cold for her to be walking every night. Alone.

"Why don't you have a car?"

"I haven't bought one since leaving the Cadillac with Clara. Besides, I like to walk."

I opened my mouth, ready to debate the safety merits of her preferred method of transportation, but I stopped myself first.

Aria would argue. I would argue. It was what we did. And tonight, with so many other important topics looming, this wasn't the argument we needed to have. So I closed my mouth and kept pace with her as she navigated us toward a two-story row of condos.

There was no need to ask which condo in the row was hers. Even in winter, she had plants on her porch while the other three condos had nothing surrounding their front doors.

Aria had two potted trees, their evergreen boughs trimmed precisely to a point. A row of red lights had been wrapped around them in a perfect spiral. Yellow lights, draped from the porch's beam, decorated the space. In the corner, a huge pot held a bush. Its red holly berries decorated the thick green leaves.

Aria slid her key in the door's lock and pushed inside. One step past the threshold and her scent enveloped me.

Sweet flowers. A hint of vanilla. *Aria.* I dragged in a long breath and let the warmth of her home chase away the chill.

She shrugged off her coat, taking it into the living room and tossing it on the back of a cream couch. Inside was like stepping into another world. Sheer white curtains covered the dark windows. There were plants everywhere, most varying shades of green but some with flowers. Red and pink poinsettias decorated the dining table. A bouquet of yellow roses flourished on the kitchen counter. With the light walls and neutral furniture shades, it was like a bungalow tucked away on a quiet island.

Serene. There was no other way to describe it. She'd made herself a haven.

And I was going to beg her to give it all up.

"Would you like some water?" she asked.

"Please."

"Make yourself comfortable." She waved to the living room, then disappeared into the kitchen and turned on the faucet.

I paced in front of the couch, unable to sit. The flight to Oregon had been brutal enough, trapped in a seat, itching to get out. Not even a fifteen-hour flight to Australia had felt so long.

Clara had been texting me all afternoon. My phone buzzed in my pocket, but I ignored it. I hadn't told her where I was going when I'd rushed out of the office. We'd been in the middle of a weekly planning meeting when

Aria had called. Clara didn't take many personal calls during our workday unless they came from August's school or her sister.

When Clara had handed me the phone, I'd thought Aria had finally decided to tell me what a prick I was for leaving after our night together. I'd been expecting it for months. I'd deserved it for months.

But pregnant? No. We'd used condoms. Multiple condoms.

I'd replayed our night together for two months. Never had it occurred to me that one of them had failed. Never. Or maybe I'd been too wrapped up in the woman to notice.

"Here." Aria came toward me, thrusting a glass of water in my hand.

I took it and gulped it to the bottom. "Thanks."

She sat down on the couch, her shoulders curling inward. "We used condoms."

"I was just thinking the same thing." I sighed, taking the chair across from her. "I didn't know that one had broken."

"This is a lot."

"Yeah."

"Not what you expected from a one-night stand, huh?"

I'd had one-night stands. My night with Aria didn't even come close to hitting that bucket. "Sorry. For leaving after the wedding."

"Why are you sorry? It was just a hookup."

Was it? Because it sure as hell didn't feel like a hookup. Definitely not with a baby on the way.

I'd been a coward for leaving without a word. She'd be right to call me on it. But I'd been scared. No woman in my life, not even Heather, had affected me like Aria. One night with her and I'd wanted more.

But this was not the time for a romantic entanglement. Certainly not a long-distance relationship. The company needed my focus if I was going to keep Grandmother from sinking the ship.

So I'd hopped on a plane the morning after Aria had snuck out of my bed—I'd woken up pissed that she'd already left—and flown back to Vegas, where I'd spent two weeks living in a hotel and working from dawn to dusk.

"Why did you come all the way here?" she asked.

"I own a plane. And I just . . . I couldn't stay in Arizona. I couldn't do this over the phone."

She tensed, studying my face. "I'm keeping this baby."

"Did you think I'd come here and ask you to have an abortion?"

"Yes."

I flinched. She might as well have slapped me. "I would never do that."

"I don't know you, Brody." Aria's voice gentled. "Not really. I just don't know what to expect from you. But I don't want to fight. I don't have the energy for it. So please don't take offense. I honestly don't know why you're here."

That was the thing with Aria, the reason her company was so refreshing. She didn't want anything from me. She didn't care about my money. She didn't care about my business. She was simply honest. Sometimes, brutally so.

Honesty, I could deliver.

"I'm here because I want to be involved. With this— our, my—baby. I won't forsake my child."

Aria blinked, her eyebrows coming together. "Seriously?"

"Is that so hard to believe?" Did she really think I was such a cold monster? Probably. And I couldn't blame her for it.

"I don't know what to believe," she whispered.

"Believe that I see how hard Clara works to raise August on her own. Believe that I don't want my child growing up without me in his or her life. Please . . . don't shut me out from this."

Now it was her turn to flinch. An expression of sheer annoyance, distinctly Aria, added fire to those tired eyes. "I would never do that."

The tension eased from my shoulders. "On the way here, I had some time to think."

"I can already tell I'm not going to like this."

A grin tugged at my mouth. "Hear me out."

She leaned back, sagging into the couch. She yawned and covered it up with her hand. "I'm listening."

"You live in Oregon."

"I do?"

"Smart-ass," I muttered. "I live in Arizona. Traveling back and forth isn't going to work, for either of us. And I am guessing that you won't want to be away from the baby for extended stretches of time."

"No. I won't."

"Then one of us has to move."

"You mean me." She sat straight, her spine stiffening. "My life is here, Brody. My work. My home. I'm not giving it all up to live in the *desert*."

The way she spat the last word made me pause. "What's wrong with the desert?"

"It's a desert."

It was too much like California.

Clara had once told me the reason she suspected Aria had run from Vegas to Oregon hadn't been the fake people or the city life, but because she'd wanted to get away from anything that reminded her of life at the junkyard in Temecula.

"You move here," she said.

"I can't." I held up my hand when she opened her mouth. "I can't in the next year."

"After that?"

"It's a possibility."

"Why a year?"

I stood from the chair and stripped off my suit coat. If we were going to get into this, we might as well get comfortable. "Are you sure you don't want dinner?"

"I could eat. How about pizza?"

Pizza. Not exactly something I ate much of. Ron normally prepared all my meals, tailoring them to my personal trainer's specifications. Ron did not make pizza. And pizza sounded fucking awesome. "That would be great."

She pulled out her phone, quickly placing an order for delivery. Then she tucked it away and gave me her attention as I resumed my seat.

"In less than a year, I'll be thirty-five. My family's company, Carmichael Communications, will become mine."

"It isn't now?"

"Only partly. At the moment, the majority of my shares are governed by a trust. My grandmother is the executor and acting owner. But the stipulations on my trust disappear on my birthday in November. Until then, I have to play her game. Otherwise she'll sell the company from under me. She'll sell it before *I* can sell it."

"Wait." Aria held up a finger. "She wants to sell your company. But you want to sell your company. Spell it out for me, Carmichael. I'm too tired to read between the lines."

"It's complicated." In a word. "Grandmother likes control. Maybe she's bluffing but maybe she's not. Selling the company is her threat. It's the reason she can demand I show up at a wedding."

"Ahh." Aria nodded. "She'd sell it out of spite."

"Exactly. And in doing so, almost every employee would lose their job."

"They wouldn't if *you* sold it?"

I shook my head. "Not if I find the right buyer. Carmichael Communications is a small player in the scope of telecommunications companies, but that doesn't mean we don't have some pull. If I sold or partnered with a larger company, we could turn it into something that might change the world."

There were innovative companies looking to acquire resources like the ones we had at Carmichael. Our research and development team had made some amazing tech in the area of satellite communications and internet capabilities.

"How does all of this require you live in Arizona?"

"We have a small R&D office in Welcome along with a data warehouse. I've moved my best employees out of Vegas to Arizona, where I can focus our efforts on the developments that position us for the big sale. If I leave Welcome, my grandmother will insist we shut the site down and move it all back to Vegas. I don't want her to know what we're doing. So far, I've managed to keep it quiet. It works because I'm there. She trusts that my incentives are to make the company flourish. After all, I'm inheriting it. That's why my grandfather set it up that way in the first place."

Aria frowned. "Complicated. I'm not a fan of your grandmother."

"You and me both. But I have to play nice. It's a game I can't lose."

"I don't play games."

No, she didn't. "My grandmother is the most tenacious woman you'll ever meet. Her greatest pleasure is control. Like I said, maybe she's bluffing. But there are hundreds of employees, including your sister, who can't take the chance that she's not."

Aria closed her eyes. "What a mess."

"You have no idea."

"And your brother? Is he part of the mess too?"

"He's never worked at Carmichael. Probably because he never got along with my grandfather."

"But you did?"

"In a way." My relationship with Grandfather hadn't been one of love and loyalty. He had been just as ruthless as Grandmother, probably why their marriage had lasted. He hadn't liked Alastair because my brother was lazy and entitled.

Aria blew out a long breath. "Arizona."

"I know it's a lot to ask." I leaned my elbows on my knees. I'd drop to them if need be. "Please. Consider it. I don't . . . I don't want my—our—child hating me because I wasn't there."

There hadn't been many times in my life when I'd needed a parent—I'd always been fairly self-sufficient and, after all, I'd had employees as my keepers. But there'd been a handful of times when I'd wanted a parent sitting in the auditorium, like my high school and college graduations. To this day, I resented them for their absence.

I refused to be that kind of father.

Aria's gaze softened. Maybe she'd heard the truth in my words. She'd realized it was a confession of the life I'd lived. And there was sympathy in her eyes because her parents hadn't been there either.

"Let me think about it," she said. "Let me see what kind of work I can find."

"You don't—"

She held up a hand. "I have to work."

"Then how about you run my flower shop?" The words spewed out before I could catch them. *Jesus, Brody.* What the hell was I thinking? The lie spun in front of my eyes, like a spider weaving a strand of silk, its legs moving faster and faster. The idea formed like a web, ready to trap Aria. For her own good.

"What flower shop?" Her eyebrows creased together.

"I just bought the local flower shop when the owners retired." Lie. "I often buy businesses in Welcome." That was true at least. If she talked to Clara, her sister would confirm it.

When a local store was getting ready to close or the owners retire, as long as the finances made sense, I bought it. Not only were they usually good investments, but it ensured my town, my safe haven, thrived.

I employed a business manager to oversee them all and

gladly stayed silent. I owned three restaurants, two bars, an insurance agency, a salon and a gym.

And now Welcome Floral.

Not that the owners of Welcome Floral knew this. Hopefully they'd be willing to sell it to me on short notice for a ridiculous price. If they didn't go for it, well . . . I'd think of something. As long as I got Aria to Welcome, the rest didn't matter.

"A year. Give me a year," I begged. "After my birthday and after the baby is born, we can come up with a new plan."

"I won't have this baby for months. Seven of them, I think. I haven't been to the doctor yet. By the time that's over and we get through a maternity leave, that should be close to your birthday. Why move? Why not just wait?"

"Because I'd miss the pregnancy."

She blinked. "I didn't think men cared about that."

"*Devan* didn't care about that." I spat the name. "I'm nothing like Devan."

"I guess not."

"Think about it. That's all I ask. Consider it." *Please.*

She nodded. "Okay."

"Thanks," I breathed and stood, pulling on my jacket. "I'll leave you to it."

"What about pizza?"

"I'll get dinner at the hotel." My stomach was in too much of a knot to eat, even though pizza sounded delicious. But if I stayed, chances were Aria and I would find something to fight about. Best I get out and end this conversation on a good note.

"You're staying?"

"Aren't you going to Arizona tomorrow for Christmas?"

"That was the plan."

"Might as well cancel your flight. There's no point in flying commercial when I'm going to the same place."

She frowned, like she wanted to argue, but she'd been on my plane. It was nothing like flying commercial. "What time are we leaving?"

"I'll pick you up at ten."

"No, don't. I'll come to the hotel."

"All right." I walked for the door, but before I touched the knob, I stopped and turned. "I know this probably seems strange, the urgency. Why I want to be there. I didn't have a good father. And I vowed a long time ago not to make the same mistakes that he made."

"You don't have to explain it to me, Brody."

"Yes, I do."

"Okay," she whispered. "Good night."

"Good night." I took one last look at her face, memorizing the contours of her cheeks and the shape of her mouth.

Her image had dulled some, since the wedding. Now it was fresh. Mesmerizing.

Fuck, but I'd missed it.

Without another word, I left, making it halfway down

the block when I saw the pizza delivery car zooming up the road. As I strode down the sidewalk, I pulled out my phone and called Clara.

"Did she kick you out yet?" she asked.

"Not yet."

"What are you doing, Brody? You're freaking out, aren't you?"

"Yes."

She sighed. "Give it time to sink in. You two will figure it out. Long-distance parenting isn't ideal, but it's not impossible."

Long-distance parenting was not an option. "I need a favor. It's going to require you hide some details from your sister."

"I don't hide things from my sister."

"Do you want her to live in Arizona?"

"Well . . . yes."

"Then that's the price."

She hesitated. In the background, a cartoon played on the TV. "Tell me."

"Tomorrow morning, I need you to buy Welcome Floral."

"What? It's not for sale."

"Everything is for sale." A truth I believed to the marrow. "Make the Backers an offer they can't refuse."

CHAPTER EIGHT

ARIA

"You're joking," Mark said. "Right?"

"I'm not."

"No." His face fell. "You can't leave."

In all the years I'd known him, I'd never seen such sorrow on his face. And disappointment. I'd come in today to give my notice as head groundskeeper at The Gallaway. Mark had been in his office and I'd asked Andy if he had a moment. Better to tell them both at the same time.

"But . . . why?" Andy asked, standing beside Mark's desk. He had one hand on the surface, holding tight like he was about to faint.

Telling them the truth, that I was pregnant, wasn't an option. Not only did that seem cruel to Andy, but considering it was still early, I wasn't sure if it was smart to make the announcement.

Plus they'd ask questions about the father I wasn't ready to answer.

"I want to live closer to my sister and nephew. He's getting older and I want to be a part of his life. Both their lives." It wasn't a lie. It was just one slice of the truth pie.

Mark blinked, staring at me like this was some sort of hoax.

"But . . ." Andy shook his head, like he was trying to rewind the last ten minutes.

"I'm so grateful," I told Mark. "You've given me the career of my dreams. Please know that I'm so very grateful. But I need to be closer to family. I'm lonely."

Understanding crossed his features. Mark had been single for as long as I'd known him. Aside from the occasional girlfriend, he lived a solitary life. But he had family in the area and he often spent time with his parents. He knew I was alone here and that I was desperately close to Clara.

"How long can you stay?" he asked.

"Two months?" That was six weeks longer than the standard notice, but I owed them a lot. And two months here would give me time to pack my condo.

Last night, Brody had asked me for a year. Only a year. But in my heart, I felt the goodbye. When I left Oregon, I wouldn't be moving back.

"Could we work out an arrangement?" Andy asked. "More time off so you can travel. Expand your staff so you're not so tied here during the season. Before you quit, let's brainstorm."

I sighed. It came as no surprise that Andy had the energy for a debate, but I was simply too tired. And nauseous. Last night's pizza was churning in my stomach. I wouldn't make it through brainstorming without puking in Mark's trash can.

Mark and I had been through a lot over the years. We'd grown to know one another as friends, not just boss and employee. But puking in the owner and CEO's trash can was crossing a line. I had minutes, not hours, before I'd need to hightail it to the bathroom.

Besides, after staying up most of the night considering Brody's proposal, any negotiation would be pointless.

I'd made my decision.

Mark must have seen the conviction on my face because he held up a hand to silence Andy. Then he gave me a sad smile. "Two months is very generous. We'll take it."

"Thank you." My shoulders slumped. So did Andy's. "For everything. Thank you."

"You'll always have a place here," he said. "If Arizona doesn't work out, come back to us."

"I appreciate that. I'll put together a transition plan and make sure the staff is trained. We're in good shape at the greenhouse."

"Don't worry about that this week." Mark waved it off.

"Go to Arizona. Enjoy Christmas. We'll plan when you return."

He really was the world's best boss's boss. I was going to miss Mark. I was going to miss The Gallaway. This job had been an anchor, keeping me grounded while I'd grown from a young woman into an adult.

And now I was going to become a mother.

I was to become the anchor.

God, I hoped I had the strength.

"Merry Christmas," I told them both, then left them alone. I closed the door behind me, but not soon enough to miss Andy release a pained groan.

Poor guy.

I breathed deeply, something I hadn't done all morning. Then the shaking set in and reality hit. It was done. I'd quit my job.

The urge to cry came on so strong I struggled to blink the tears away as I walked down the hallway, making my way to the main floor. But there wasn't time to cry. Because I had to puke.

After a quick stop at the bathroom—at least I was getting used to the retching—I went to the lobby. Mark and Andy had been my first stop of the day. Brody was the second.

"Hey," I greeted the receptionist. "Could you ring a guest room for me?"

"Sure. What's the name?"

"Bro—" The call wasn't necessary. As I glanced over

my shoulder, I spotted him in the lobby. "Oh. Never mind."

Brody stood in the center of the room, dressed in the same suit he'd worn last night, talking on the phone. He looked rumpled. His hair was damp and finger combed. His suit wasn't its usual crisp. Still, he was the most handsome man to ever grace these halls.

He'd come here without a bag, hadn't he? The cold robot who loved money had cared enough and been freaked out enough to hop on a plane without so much as a toothbrush. He'd come here on a spur-of-the-moment decision because our lives were now different. Entwined.

He'd rushed to my side and begged me not to cut him out of our kid's life.

Brody never stopped surprising me.

It was endearing, seeing him as human, knowing he wasn't abandoning me to single parenthood. His apology for the morning after the wedding had helped too.

Hovering beside the reception counter, I waited until he hung up the phone. He let his arm drop, the device in his grip, but he stared at it like he wanted to throw it on the floor and walk away forever.

Brody dragged a hand through his hair, tucked the phone into his pocket and turned. He took one step before his chin lifted and he spotted me. Then he froze.

"Hi." I waved and crossed the lobby.

"Hi. How are you?" Brody towered over me, seeming taller than ever today, even disheveled.

Was it strange that I wanted him to hold me?

"Nauseated. Tired. Soon to be unemployed."

He blinked. "Unemployed."

I nodded toward the hallway. "Walk with me."

Without a protest, he fell into step at my side as I led him through the hotel, stopping by the locker room for my coat, then out an employee exit. Then we hoofed it in the chilly weather to the greenhouse.

Like yesterday, it was empty, most of the staff on vacation for the upcoming holiday. The ones working were at the hotel. We strolled past the long tables and into the area with the seedlings I'd planted yesterday. Someone had watered them this morning.

I pulled out a wooden stool and shrugged off my coat. Then I gestured for Brody to sit in the other stool. "I thought about what you had to say."

"And you quit your job."

"I don't know what I'm doing," I confessed. "I'm winging it and picking the option that feels right. This, moving to Arizona, seems less scary than raising a baby here alone. And I'm tired of feeling lonely."

That was the second time I'd admitted it today. Now that the word *lonely* was out there, I was having a hard time hiding from it.

"I don't want this baby to be lonely," I said. "Family is important and living close to Clara and August has been something on my mind for a while now. I'd hoped to convince her to move here but . . . we'll try Arizona."

Brody's entire face changed. Gone was the fear and worry. Gone was the stoic, stony gaze. Everything melted. His eyes. The hold of those soft lips. His shoulders dropped from his ears. He almost looked . . . happy. He looked like the man who'd charmed me at a wedding.

"Thank you."

"I can't promise it's forever. But I can give you the year."

He took one of my hands in both of his, his palms warming my skin. He pressed it, my hand sandwiched between his, and he dropped his chin. "Thank you."

"What did you expect me to say?"

"No. I thought you'd say no."

"I almost did," I admitted. "Last night, I thought about what you said. And I thought about what I wanted. Arizona is not what I want."

I wanted to live here in my cozy condo. I wanted to keep my job at The Gallaway because it was dependable. I wanted to avoid turning my life upside down. But if I'd wanted all that, then I shouldn't have had sex with Brody.

If only he'd been resistible.

"But it's not about me. And it's not about you," I said, splaying my free hand over my belly. "It's about this baby. I don't want our child to feel torn between two worlds."

Brody had the right to be included in this baby's life. He was as much a part of this as I was.

"I promised my boss two months. I'd like to give them

a chance for a smooth transition, and I need to pack up my life here."

Brody stared at me, my hand still tight between his. The shock on his face was much like Mark's. Apparently, I was surprising the men in my life today.

"Is that okay?"

He dropped my hand and, in a flash, those warm palms were on my face, pulling me off my stool. Brody's lips crushed mine, sending a zing down my spine. God, his lips were soft. The texture from his beard tickled my chin, and when his tongue darted out to lick the seam of my mouth, a whole new flutter rocked my stomach. This one the good kind.

A gasp escaped when he licked my lips again. His eyes opened.

And we stared at one another, our lips still locked. His hands still firm on my face.

As quickly as it happened, Brody must have realized what he'd done. He let me go and backed away, clearing his throat. "I, uh . . . Thank you."

Disappointment rolled over me in a wave, sending me back to my seat.

There was no reason to be upset, right? It was just a grateful kiss. Nothing romantic. The two of us would be lucky to survive parenthood together. A romantic relationship? Never. We really shouldn't be kissing.

"You're welcome. Maybe we shouldn't make a habit of kissing one another."

He chuckled. "Sorry. I was excited. But you're right. Let's think of this as business."

"Business." I truly hated that word. People tossed it out there as an excuse to be cold and impersonal. "This is not a business arrangement."

"Of course it is."

My mouth dropped. "Seriously?"

"You'll be running my new flower shop. That's business. I mean, it's not like we're friends."

My jaw dropped. "So you think of me like an employee?" Oh, hell. Maybe I'd quit The Gallaway too soon. Mark and Andy would hire me back, right?

Brody frowned. "You say that like being an employee of mine is a nightmare. I doubt your sister would agree."

"I am not your employee."

"I know that but—"

"No buts. We are equals, Brody. You're the father. I'm the mother. I don't need your goddamn flower shop. I can find another job. Any other job." My temperature began to rise and I slid off my stool, pacing beside the table.

"Aria, I'm just being pragmatic. Please don't take offense. I have a flower shop that needs a manager. You're qualified."

"Qualified. I'm qualified." My molars ground together. When had this become a job interview? "I won't work for you."

"Why not?"

"Because that makes this entire thing weird." I threw

up my hands. Couldn't he imagine payday? *Here's your check, Aria. Thanks for your hard work. And thanks for growing my baby in your uterus.*

"If you don't like the term 'employee,' then fine. I'll deed the place over to you."

"A gift. You'd give me a flower shop." My hands dove into my hair. "Who does that?"

We weren't even friends. We'd slept together once and were having a kid. Normal people didn't gift flower shops.

He lifted a shoulder. "You're moving. Consider it a relocation present. And it's not like I can't afford it."

"There." I pointed to the arrogant jerk's face. "That, right there."

"What, right there?" He rubbed the tip of his nose, checking his fingers to see if there was something on them.

"That, right there, is the reason I hate you. You throw money around like it's meaningless. Don't try to buy me."

"I'm not trying to buy you." He frowned. "I'm trying to make this easy on you. On both of us. If you want the flower shop, it's yours."

"What if . . ." I snapped my fingers. "What if I bought it from you?"

"It's unnecessary."

"How much did you pay for it?"

His jaw ticked, the hold on his patience slipping. "Why does it matter?"

"How. Much?"

"One hundred and twenty-five thousand dollars."

Well, shit. I didn't have anywhere near that much in savings. But maybe I had enough for a down payment.

I held out my hand. "Deal."

"What deal?"

"The flower shop. I'll buy it from you. If you will accept monthly payments."

Brody shook his head. "That's not the point of this. I came here to ask you to move. I'm not going to put you in debt because of it."

"Then we'll make the monthly payments manageable." I wiggled the fingers of my outstretched hand, waiting for him to accept.

"Aria—"

"I won't budge on this. I won't be a charity case."

He sighed. "It's not charity."

"It feels like it to me."

Brody's mouth flattened because I'd just won. "I won't have the monthly payment become a burden. This cannot be something that causes you stress."

"Life is stressful."

"But it shouldn't be for you."

The gentleness in his voice tempered my anger. "Okay."

He took my hand in his, sealing the deal.

I'd bought a flower shop. *Oh my God*. I'd just bought a flower shop.

The dream. It was my dream. And my head was spinning so fast I wasn't sure if I should cry or laugh. It was too much, all of these changes were too much. I was in the middle of an ocean during a hurricane, and the seasickness was overwhelming.

If I looked too far into the future, the uncertainty would crumple me to my knees.

One day at a time. That's all I had in me at the moment. One moment. One step. One day at a time.

I was moving to Arizona. I was buying a flower shop. I was becoming a mother.

I'd tackle them each, starting with the first, but not today.

"Now what?" Brody asked, seeming as lost as I was.

I shrugged. "How about that ride to Arizona? I have some Christmas presents to deliver."

CHAPTER NINE

BRODY

"Where is she?" I checked my phone for the tenth time.

"You're worse than August," Clara muttered.

Not quite. August was outside, bundled in a coat and hat for the cooler February weather, driving his child-size Jeep around the driveway. Circle after circle, his eyes were locked on the entry gate.

Mine were too.

We were both anxious for her to arrive.

I paced in front of the window. "This is fucking ridiculous."

"So you've said." Clara sat on the couch in my living room, her eyes locked on her phone. She'd been pinning recipes and baby outfits on Pinterest—I'd asked what had her so enraptured when she should be worrying about Aria.

Aria, the obstinate, exasperating woman who had refused to let me hire her a moving company. Aria, my pregnant—*friend? associate? acquaintance?*—someone, who had insisted on packing her own belongings and loading them into a U-Haul to drive from Oregon to Arizona.

Would she let me fly up to help her? No.

Would she let me hire someone to drive the truck so she could fly here on my jet? No.

Would she listen to reason that a pregnant woman should not be lifting boxes and hefting houseplants? No.

Aria hadn't even let her sister come to Oregon and help when Clara had offered.

There wasn't a more stubborn woman on planet Earth than Aria Saint-James. In the past two months, she'd pushed me to the brink of sanity.

"Never in my life have I met a person so inflexible as your sister."

Clara scoffed. "Then you need to look in the mirror."

"What?" I spun away from the glass. "I'm not inflexible."

That earned me an eye roll. "If it's not your way, then it's the wrong way. Did you ever think that maybe Aria needed to do this herself? That she needed some time on the road to say goodbye to her old life? She loves surprises and spontaneity, but that doesn't mean she hasn't let her roots grow deep."

"If she needed time, I would have given her time. All I

asked is that she not drive a rental truck from Heron Beach to Welcome by herself."

"We lived in a junkyard, Brody. We were fifteen. Alone. Broke. Aria's not scared of a two-day drive."

I opened my mouth to argue but clamped it shut. Maybe I didn't give Aria enough credit.

It was her beauty that made me forget about their childhood and all she'd endured. When she smiled and laughed, it was like she'd lived the happiest life in the world. Aria was strong, I knew that. So was Clara. Still . . . "I just want to help her. Make this easier."

I had the means to make her life simpler. She'd called it charity. Why couldn't she see it as generosity? What the fuck else was I supposed to spend my money on if not the woman who was carrying my child? How was offering to find her work and a home charity? I'd be an asshole if I let her fend for herself.

"You didn't tell her about the flower shop, right?" I asked.

"No," Clara said. "My answer hasn't changed since you asked me yesterday. And the day before that. And for all the days before that over the past two months."

I frowned. "I know you don't like to keep secrets from her."

"When she finds out, she'll be furious. At both of us."

"*If* she finds out."

Clara laughed. "You don't know Aria very well. I

promised you I wouldn't tell her but that doesn't mean she won't find out. She has a way of sniffing out secrets."

"She can't find out." The contract had a nondisclosure clause in place to ensure my secret was safe. And the previous owners were in Hawaii. Gone for good, so the chances of it slipping were slim to none.

Welcome Floral hadn't cost me one hundred and twenty-five thousand dollars like I'd told Aria. No, the flower shop had cost me four hundred and eighty thousand dollars. Nearly half a million.

I had to hand it to the previous owners, the ruthless bastards. Ned and Stephanie Backer had smelled my desperation and pounced like lions on a wounded gazelle. But my payment had meant they could retire in Hawaii, far from Aria's prying ears.

It would take Aria a lifetime to pay for the floral shop at the Backers' price tag. Hell, even with the *discount* price I'd quoted her it would be a lot. I'd seen the financial statements from the flower shop and Aria had some work to do if she wanted to turn a larger monthly profit.

But it was a solid business. She'd own the building downtown, and I hoped that after a year in Welcome, she'd realize my small town wasn't without its charms.

I'd meant what I'd told her. After my birthday, I'd consider moving. But I also liked it here in Arizona. I loved this lifeless house. It was safe. Comfortable. Ron had his bungalow on the property. Clara had her house. One day, I wanted to see my child outside playing in the driveway.

If Aria insisted on moving, I'd move. But I had nearly a year to get those roots of hers to sink into the desert sand.

I checked my watch again, wondering for the thousandth time where she was. Aria had promised to be here no later than two, so where the hell was she? It was two thirty, and if she didn't get here within the next fifteen minutes, I was going out to search.

The text message I'd sent her had gone unanswered.

Aria and I hadn't spoken much over the past two months. Most of our communication either went through Clara or was via text. How we were going to live together was a mystery.

It was the one thing about this move—other than the destination—Aria had conceded without a fight. She was moving into my house.

Clara had offered her guest room but Aria had told me during a rare phone conversation that she didn't want to invade her sister's life. When I'd offered her my place, a stone's throw from Clara and August plus more space than she'd find in a local rental, she'd shocked me by agreeing.

It would be the first time I'd lived with a woman. Not even Heather had occupied my space. I'd never invited her to move in. The weekends when she'd slept over had been bad enough. Makeup all over the bathroom counter. Clothes strewn on the floor for the housekeeper to pick up. Yes, I paid my staff to do that very thing, but for fuck's sake, the laundry basket had been twenty feet away in the closet.

Thankfully this house was much larger than my Vegas penthouse, and I wouldn't be sharing a bed. Aria would occupy one end of the house with me in the opposite. If she was sloppy or loud, I'd be too far away to notice.

"I'm going to wait outside," Clara said. "Your pacing is making me nervous."

Was I pacing? I stopped midstride. "Fifteen minutes and I'm going to go look for her."

Clara shook her head. "I'm going to give you some unsolicited advice about Aria."

"Okay," I drawled. For the most part, other than playing messenger for logistical details, Clara had stayed far away from the mess that was Aria and me. Though I wasn't foolish enough to think that if push came to shove, she'd choose me over her sister.

But when we spoke of Aria, Clara maintained a neutral stance. She relayed facts. She let me rant without much commentary. And she didn't offer more than a shred of insight into the mysterious woman who had consumed my waking thoughts. Until now.

"Aria needs control in her life. After Mom and Dad died, she became the sister in charge. I didn't . . . She didn't fall apart. I did."

My heart twisted as I stood frozen, watching her struggle with whatever she was going to say. Clara didn't speak much about that time. Or about her time in the junkyard. She'd told me the big picture, but any details had been glossed over. Clara had told me facts. Dates. Nothing more.

And the cold asshole that I was, I had never asked how she'd actually felt.

Now, with Aria coming here, I wanted to know. To truly know what their youth had been like. We were a family of sorts, tied together by this unexpected baby.

"It was Aria's idea to run away from our uncle's home."

"Why?" What had happened with her uncle that had been so terrible that a desolate life in a junkyard had been the better option? "What happened?"

Something crossed Clara's gaze, a sadness deeper than anything I'd ever seen before. "You'll have to ask Aria."

I frowned. "If you won't tell me, she certainly won't."

"Give it time." She gave me a watery smile. "Don't take her freedom, Brody. Don't take her control."

"I'm trying to help."

"No, you're keeping *your* control. You need to find a way where you can both have it."

"Share," I grumbled. I'd hated the word *share* since kindergarten.

"Yes." She laughed. "You have to share."

I turned my back to her, facing the glass. When she walked outside to join her son, I resumed my pacing. It was the only way to keep my vibrating nerves from shaking my bones loose. This restless energy had plagued me since Aria had told me she was pregnant. I'd paced a lot since.

I was becoming a father.

Christ. What had I gotten myself into? It would be easy to blame it on the champagne. I didn't drink often, certainly not like I had at the wedding. But it hadn't been a drunken haze. It had been Aria.

Sitting on my counter in that stunning green dress, her feet bare, she'd rendered me helpless. One kiss and I'd been lost.

Lost in her mouth, her hands, her taste. Four months later and I couldn't get that night out of my head. Her body, sleek and tight, had been a dream. Moving inside her, hovering above her, had been the best sex of my life.

"Don't," I told myself. It had been a constant reminder over the past couple months.

Sex could not, would not, enter into this arrangement. Aria and I had a tumultuous relationship at best. Somehow, we had to forge a truce. A friendship would be ideal, but I'd settle for civility.

I just wanted my kid to know me. That was it. Simple. I didn't need love and adoration. I just wanted knowledge.

Liar. I couldn't even fool myself.

I wanted love. I wanted my son or daughter to think I was the best man in the world. There was no way I'd pull it off. But that wouldn't stop me from trying. How was I supposed to be a good father? There hadn't been a kind and gentle male influence in my life. What did I know about raising a child?

I breathed and swallowed the fears. The insecurities would attack later. Probably for the rest of my life.

Down the driveway, something flickered. I stood straighter, leaning closer to the glass as a white and orange truck emerged. My heart leapt into my throat as I rushed from the window, jogging for the front door. I flung it open and hurried outside, joining Clara in the driveway. August was racing down the concrete, his arms waving as he screeched, "Aunt Aria!"

She honked, the noise more of a muted bark than a blare. Her smile beamed from behind the wheel as she eased the truck to a stop with an ear-splitting squeal of its brakes.

"*That* is the truck she rented?"

"Shut it." Clara elbowed me in the ribs, then rushed for the driver's side door as Aria shoved it open.

Her feet had barely hit the ground before Clara had her in a hug. The two of them held on to one another as August crashed into their sides.

And I stood back, watching.

I wanted to be in that hug. I wanted to be included. Where had that longing come from? It niggled but I shoved it away. When had I turned into such a damn sap? Carmichaels didn't hug.

Aria let Clara go and turned my way. "Hi."

"Hi." I cleared my throat. "You're late."

The woman had the gall to laugh. Then she slammed the door shut on the U-Haul and moseyed my way. Her dark hair was lighter than it had been at Christmas. She'd added streaks of a dark blond that highlighted the flecks of gold in her eyes. The dark circles under her eyes were gone. The rosy color in her cheeks matched the pink pout of her mouth.

A surge of lust shot straight to my groin. *Fuck*. This was not the time.

"Be grumpy later," she said, patting my stomach as she marched past me for the house. "We have work to do."

Clara pulled in her lips to hide a smile as she passed me, following her sister.

I looked to the blue sky and dragged in a deep breath. If they knew why I was *grumpy*, they'd have an entirely different reaction. Getting a grip on this attraction to Aria was taking more effort than I'd expected.

August raced past me, following his mother and aunt. "Come on, Brody!"

"Coming," I muttered, taking a moment with my back turned to adjust my swelling cock. Then I turned and met them in the house.

Aria was looking around, surveying the space. "It's bigger than I remember."

"Are you feeling okay?"

She dropped her gaze and smiled. "I'm good. Much better. The morning sickness has pretty much disappeared now."

"Good. Can I get you some water or juice or—"

"Here you are, sir." Ron appeared, carrying a tray from the kitchen filled with glasses of ice and sparkling water, each with a lemon wedge on the rim.

"Thank you, Ron." I took a glass, then handed one to both Aria and Clara. August received a juice box.

"Cheers." Clara raised her glass. "To a new adventure."

"Cheers." Aria clinked glasses with her sister, then with mine before taking a long drink. If she felt uncomfortable about being here, it didn't show. This was the woman who'd waltzed into a wedding full of strangers and held her chin high the entire time.

"The crew will be here in fifteen minutes," Ron said.

"Excellent. I—"

"Crew. What crew?" Aria asked.

"The crew to unpack."

"Oh, we don't need a crew. I don't have much. You can just cancel them."

"But—" One pointed look from Clara and I cut myself off. Control. Aria needed control. It went against my nature, but I could let this one go. "All right. Cancel them, Ron."

"Yes, sir." He tucked his now-empty tray under an arm and disappeared.

"Let me show you around." I gestured for them to follow me deeper into the house, toward the wing that would become Aria's. "I don't spend much time in these rooms. I stick to my office, bedroom and the gym, so I won't bother you. You've got complete run of the place. Please make this your home."

"I don't need much space."

She'd have it regardless.

We walked down a hallway that led toward the back of the house. Windows made up the exterior walls, as they did in the entire place. She'd have a view of the desert property that surrounded us on all sides.

This side of the house had five bedrooms. There was an office for her on the second floor as well as a sitting room with a fireplace. I escorted her to the largest bedroom first, opening the door to the room. Along one wall was a king-sized bed with a white canopy and ivory quilt. I'd had the gossamer draping added just last week.

The walls, once midnight blue, had been repainted a soft cream. The hardwood floors had been refinished and restained from the pale gray she'd objected to the night of the wedding. Their honey-colored grains emitted a warm glow in the space. The fawn and mushroom area rug beneath the bed was so plush that even I'd tried it beneath my bare feet—then I'd ordered one for my own bedroom.

At Christmas, we hadn't broached the topic of where she'd live. That vacation had been awkward at best. Aria and Clara had invited me over for Christmas dinner, and the moment the meal had finished, I'd retreated to my office. The evening had been pleasant, but Aria had left me unsettled. Her stare from across the table had been unnerving, like she'd seen my fears about the pregnancy.

Like she'd seen the restraint it had taken to keep from touching her shiny hair and caressing her pretty skin.

Insecurity wasn't in the Carmichael gene pool. At least, I hadn't thought so until Aria and this baby had proved me wrong.

After Christmas, she'd returned to Oregon and I'd hired a designer to rework the bedrooms. They now had the light, bright and airy feel that I'd seen in her condo. The only things missing were the plants.

No doubt those were in the U-Haul.

"Um . . . this is not what I expected." Aria blinked, her eyes wide as she stepped into the space. She had her own walk-in closet. An en suite bathroom. And a pair of french doors that opened to the pool outside.

"Brody had it redesigned," Clara announced.

Aria looked all around the room, her eyes landing on me. "You didn't have to do this."

"It was no trouble. I want you to be comfortable. If you don't like it, we can—"

"I love it." She smiled, and if I'd thought the room was bright before, I'd been entirely mistaken. Her smile was luminescent.

A flutter rippled through my chest, odd and unfamiliar. Must be heartburn. "If you need anything at all, there's a call system in each room that rings directly to Ron."

"I'm fairly self-sufficient," she said.

"Just in case." I nodded toward the door. "Let me show you the rest, then we'll get the truck unloaded."

The tour took another twenty minutes. We didn't linger in the other bedrooms, one of which I'd earmarked for a nursery. Aria had instantly agreed since it was adjacent to hers. She'd taken one look at the gym and told me she wouldn't be spending much time there. Then she claimed the theater room as her own.

"I'll get changed," I said. "Meet you outside."

Aria and Clara were too busy picking out lounge chairs in front of the massive projector screen to notice when I disappeared to the opposite end of the house to change out of the navy slacks and starched white shirt I'd pulled on this morning.

When I went outside to find them, Clara met me on the sidewalk carrying a box. August trailed behind her, his arms wrapped tightly around a potted fern twice the size of his face.

Aria was in the back of the U-Haul, loosening a strap she'd used to secure boxes.

"This is it?" I counted twenty, maybe thirty boxes in total. They were all stacked to one side while the rest of the floor had plants. "What about furniture?"

"I made an agreement with my landlord to leave it furnished for a free month's rent." She shrugged, rolling the strap into a coil. "I didn't think there'd be much point trying to load up furniture myself and haul it down here when I assumed you had everything here already."

"That's why you refused a moving company."

She grinned, walking to the end of the box, towering over me. "The heaviest thing in here is a box of books. Those are marked and waiting just for you."

"Here." I held out my hands to help her down.

She grabbed them, jumping to the ground. Then she cocked her head to the side, looking me up and down.

"What?"

"You're in jeans."

I dropped my gaze to my dark-wash jeans and simple white thermal. "What's wrong with them?"

"Nothing." Her eyes twinkled. "I've just never seen you in anything but a suit."

"You've seen me naked."

"This is true." Her cheeks flushed and she pulled her bottom lip between her teeth.

Why the hell had I brought up being naked? Now all I could picture was her flawless skin when I'd stripped her of that green gown.

Aria had perfect skin, smooth and supple. It had been like silk against my palms. Her hair had threaded through my fingers like strands of the finest satin.

I raised a hand, ready to tuck a lock of hair behind her ear, then realized I'd almost touched her and froze.

Her gaze darted to my hand, stuck in midair.

An impulse. When it came to Aria, I seemed to have them constantly, like that kiss at the greenhouse. I'd never in my life kissed a woman so blindly. It hadn't been sexual or foreplay. She'd made me so happy that I'd just . . . kissed her.

Maybe I'd kiss her again. The idea should have scared the hell out of me, enough to have me racing into the house and telling Ron he had book box duty. Instead, I inched closer.

Aria's chin lifted so she could keep my gaze.

And the stray lock of hair was mine. One sweep around the shell of her ear and Aria's breath hitched.

"Aunt Aria! I'm ready for another plant!"

She jerked.

I stepped away as August rounded the corner of the truck, his arms outstretched.

"Great. Good job." She smiled at him and kept her gaze anywhere other than me. Then she found the smallest pot she could within reach and loaded it into her nephew's grip.

I ran a hand over my beard and willed my body to cool. *Get it together, Brody.* What was wrong with me today?

Aria was off-limits. A hard no. Why couldn't I seem to grasp that concept? Maybe because I didn't like the word *no*, even when I issued it myself.

I put my head down and went to work unloading the truck. The sooner I got away from Aria, the better. She'd be busy unpacking today, and I could get some space. Yes, she was beautiful. Yes, she smelled like a dream.

But she was carrying my child.

That was where this relationship had to end.

It only took an hour to empty the moving truck. While Aria, Clara and August went to return it to the local drop-off, I locked myself in my office, where I spent the remainder of the afternoon and evening.

This was the only way it would work. Aria had her half of the house. I had mine. Not wanting to risk an encounter, I had Ron deliver dinner to my desk. Not that it mattered. He informed me that Aria had gone to Clara's.

When night fell and darkness came, I finally ventured out of my office at close to midnight for some fresh air. I went to the kitchen for a glass of water, then slipped outside. The light from Aria's bedroom was off. The blue glow from the pool lit up the patio.

I padded, barefoot, to one of the chairs, hoping to spend a quiet moment looking at the stars. But that plan went to hell with a splash of water.

"Do you always work so late on a Saturday?" Aria was seated at the edge of the pool. She'd rolled up her own jeans to her knees. Her feet and calves dangled in the warm water.

"I didn't see you."

"Obviously." She laughed. "Are you done avoiding me?"

"I wasn't—" *Shit.* "Yes."

She patted the concrete space at her side. "I won't bite."

I opened my mouth to correct her, because she most

definitely did bite. I'd had the mark to prove it for two days after the wedding. But I caught myself and blocked out all memories of that night.

"Brody. Sit down."

I unglued my feet and crossed to the pool, bending to cuff my own jeans before putting my feet in the water beside hers.

Aria kicked her legs and wiggled her toes, then leaned back, using her arms as a brace, as she looked up at the sky.

Diamonds studded the endless night. The white haze of the Milky Way threaded through the stars' glowing beams.

"I used to climb on top of the delivery van at the junk-yard and look up at the stars. It's better than TV, don't you think?"

"Yes, I do." I leaned back too, taking my first deep breath. "What kind of delivery van?"

"It wasn't entirely different than the one I drove down here, though the one at the junkyard hadn't worked in years. It had gotten into an accident. The front end was all smashed and crumpled. But the box had a fairly solid floor. There were a few jagged tears and holes from the accident, but we found some plastic to cover them up. It let the sunshine in and kept the rain out. And the rodents."

I grimaced. It physically pained me to think of Aria and Clara living with mice and rats. When I'd been fifteen, I'd lived at a private school in New Hampshire.

My biggest fear hadn't been vermin or scrounging up enough money to buy a loaf of bread. I'd concerned myself with more trivial matters, like teenaged girls and acne.

"I don't like that you had to go through that."

"Me neither," she admitted. "But it wasn't that bad. I learned how to grow plants there. Clara made us these little bedrolls and shelves out of yellowed and torn books she bought for a dime at the thrift store. It became home."

And now my home was her home. "Thank you, Aria."

"You keep saying that."

"Because it deserves to be said more than once."

"You're welcome." She pressed a hand to her belly. The gray sweater she was wearing was loose and had been draped over her midsection earlier. But now that she was leaning back, I could see the faintest swell to her belly.

That was my baby in there. Mine.

"Think we'll survive this?" she asked. "Living together. Having a baby."

I took in her profile, studying the tip of her nose and the pout of her lips. Yeah, we'd survive it. If I could find a way to keep from screwing it up. Namely, by dragging her back to my bed.

Survive it?

"I hope so."

CHAPTER TEN

ARIA

W elcome Floral.

The letters etched in gold on the door's glass panel smiled at me as Brody twisted the key in the lock and we stepped inside. Above our heads, a bronze bell shaped like a lily of the valley bloom dinged.

"First impression?" Brody asked quietly.

"Not bad, Carmichael. Not bad."

The air, infused with a clean floral fragrance, wrapped me in a warm hug as the door closed behind us. The humid air plumped my dry skin. The greenery and bright colors were like taking in a long-lost friend.

I'd bought this place.

Welcome Floral.

This was mine. Or would be one day after a string of payments to Brody.

"You really like it?" he asked at my side. There was a

wary look on his face, like he was scared I'd hate it and call this entire thing off.

But I wasn't a quitter.

And Welcome Floral was my dream come true.

"It's charming."

The garden gnomes beside a large potted hosta had smiles and pink cheeks. One winked at me. Another showed me his butt cheeks. The glass display case was filled with arrangements and bouquets. I preferred clean, tight bundles to wild sprays and billowing greens, but while they weren't exactly my style, they were tasteful and bright and balanced.

An old window with foggy glass panes and a chipped frame hung above the display table to my right. A rusty bicycle dangled above the table to my left. Tin cans surrounded table legs. An antique chair held a bouquet of peach roses. The walkways were narrow and curved, forming a maze through the shop.

Shabby chic. That was the only way to describe the eclectic style. It was cute. Maybe a little cluttered, but as I'd told Brody, charming.

He checked his watch. "Marty should be here any minute."

"Okay." My nerves spiked.

Marty was the manager here. He'd worked for the previous owners for years, and during the negotiations, they'd asked Brody to keep him on.

"This is your business," he reminded me for the third time today. "You can do whatever you want."

Meaning I was free to let Marty go if we didn't get along.

But I wanted us to get along. I'd need an experienced manager when this baby came. And from what Brody had told me, Marty was not only experienced, he was afford-able. This meeting had to go well.

I hummed and walked away, letting those words sink in as I touched the tip of an Easter lily.

This was my business.

My business.

My training was geared toward landscaping and growing stock in a greenhouse. In Oregon. Now I was the owner of a floral shop in a desert. Clueless was the word that popped into mind.

My business needed a Marty.

I needed an ally.

Because so far, my few interactions with Brody had been . . . strained.

Even after our conversation by the pool, Brody had avoided me most of the day yesterday. I'd had plenty to keep busy. All of the boxes I'd brought from Oregon had been unpacked. I'd spent a nice chunk of time with Clara and August. The only time I'd seen him had been at dinner.

Brody had been seated alone at the dining room table, his meal before him, his attention on his phone. We'd exchanged a glance. I'd smiled. He'd nodded and asked me how I was feeling. Then I'd retreated to my room to sleep.

This morning I'd woken up at five. With nothing to do and my anxiety about today's visit to the shop going at full steam, I wandered around the house, trying to rid myself of nervous energy while getting oriented with the different hallways and rooms.

The noise of leather smacking leather and a few sharp breaths had stopped my feet. I'd entered Brody's part of the house. He'd been in his home gym, a space twice as large as my Oregon condo.

He'd been at a punching bag, beating the hell out of the swinging cylinder, wearing only a pair of shorts. His back and shoulders had glistened with sweat. His tennis-shoe-clad feet had skipped, light and fast like grasshoppers, over the red cushioned mat.

I'd stayed at the doorway, watching him until he'd finally dropped his gloved hands. Before he could catch me spying, I'd ducked out of sight. But not before catching a glimpse of those washboard abs in the wall of mirrors.

The man's body was a work of art. Chiseled and powerful. Graceful and strong. Brody was incredible in a suit. Truly mouthwatering. But this morning, barely clothed, I'd nearly orgasmed from the sight alone.

Pregnancy hormones were going to be a bitch.

An hour later, he'd found me in the kitchen, eating at the island. Ron, who doubled as butler and chef, had cooked me a feast. Spinach and egg white omelet. Fruit and yogurt parfait. Fresh squeezed orange juice and a homemade bran muffin.

Brody had shown up—protein shake in hand—with a set of keys and a folder full of codes and passwords. The garage, the internet, the security system. After giving me the rundown, he'd disappeared.

An hour ago, he'd summoned me to his office via text, where he'd had the official buy-sell agreement for the floral shop waiting. Clara had been there, smiling on, as I'd signed on the bottom line.

Then she'd stayed home to wait for August to get done with school for the day, while Brody had brought me here.

Welcome Floral was closed on Mondays, something I'd be changing soon enough. But today, I was glad for it. I didn't need a customer coming in during my initial meet and greet with Marty.

The door chimed behind us, and a man in his fifties with a bald head and tortoiseshell glasses perched on his freckled nose walked inside. His green, short-sleeved button-down was undone nearly to his sternum. Whatever hair he lacked on his head he made up for with curly grays peeking out from above his heart.

"Marty." Brody extended his hand. "Good afternoon."

"Afternoon." Marty's gaze traveled my way. He looked me up and down, taking in my black skinny jeans and white Adidas shoes.

The pants I couldn't button anymore, but I'd secured the button to its hole with an elastic hair tie. My flowy white tee was covered with a thick cream cardigan because Welcome was cold today. To my delight, my winter wardrobe, sans snow boots, wouldn't be completely pointless in Arizona.

"Hi." I crossed the space for the door, my hand outstretched for Marty. "I'm Aria Saint-James."

"Marty Mathers." He shook my hand, then straightened his shoulders. "I've worked here for seven years. I specialize in floral design, but I also take care of the ordering. I'm willing to do delivery if necessary, though there's a young lady who's been doing it for the past year and she'd like to keep her job. So would I."

"This isn't an interview." I gave Marty my warmest smile. "Well, maybe it is. I guess I assumed today you'd interview me and decide if you wanted to stick around and help me get my feet wet."

Marty blinked. "Oh."

Time would tell if Marty was the right fit for my long-term vision. But I'd be stupid to let him go. If the previous owners had trusted him and he'd run this place for Brody since the business had shifted hands, that was good enough for me.

"I'd like that," Marty said, relief washing over his face.

"Good."

"Water?" He pointed toward the far wall. "My throat is a little dry."

"Please and thank you."

He smiled, revealing a little gap between his front

teeth, then he moved past me and disappeared into the shop.

"Phew." I blew out a long breath and pressed a hand to my heart. "That went okay."

"Marty's a good guy. At least, that's what my business manager said. She's been working with him, checking in and such, during the transition. Marty pretty much does it all around here. I think you two will get along."

"I hope so."

"I'll leave you two to get acquainted," Brody said, taking his phone from his pocket. "I'll be in the car. Take your time."

"Thanks." I nodded as he walked out the door, giving his backside a thorough inspection.

Broad shoulders. Long, powerful legs. His suit jacket covered his ass. *Damn.* But at least I had this morning's mental image to call up and appreciate.

"He's something, isn't he?"

I jumped at Marty's voice. While I'd been ogling Brody, he'd returned with two mugs. Both brimmed with water. "Pardon?"

"Here." Marty handed me my cup. It was white and hand painted with small, bright flowers. I'd noticed the same on a display table, each selling for fifteen dollars. "He's something. Brody."

"Oh." *Busted.* "He's . . . handsome enough."

"You were undressing him with your eyes, my darling.

I get it." Marty laughed. "My husband and I both have him on our cheat list."

"You have a cheat list?"

"Of course. Why would you not have a cheat list? We know Brody's straight but my mother always said I had a penchant for grand delusions."

I giggled. "Good to know."

"Now come on back to the table so we can sit down. Then you're going to tell me all about yourself, Aria Saint-James."

"I'd like that."

Two hours later, I walked out of the floral shop with a beaming smile.

The moment he spotted me, Brody hopped out of his car and rounded the hood, meeting me at the passenger door. "How'd it go?"

"Great." I was so happy I could cry. "I love Marty."

Time had flown talking to him. Hilarious and honest and dedicated to the shop and our customers, Marty was exactly the kind of person I needed by my side. When I'd told him I was pregnant, he'd immediately assured me I could count on him to run the shop during my maternity leave. Then he'd listened intently and followed me around the shop as I'd rambled ideas.

"And the shop?" Brody asked. "Do you like it?"

"I must be insane. I bought a flower shop without ever setting foot inside."

"We can rip up the paperwork."

I shook my head. "It's perfect. I want to put my own mark on it. Change the style a bit. But I want it."

"Then it's yours." He opened the car door for me, something he'd done earlier today when we'd left the house.

"You wouldn't open the door for me before the wedding, when I was in death heels, but now that I'm in tennis shoes, you do."

"Forgive me." He feigned a dramatic bow as I took my seat. "I hadn't appreciated the precious cargo."

My cheeks flushed as he shut the door and walked to the driver's seat, getting behind the wheel. He'd been teasing too, but the comment still tasted sweet.

"You didn't need to drive me. I could have come down myself."

"In what car?" Brody asked, driving us through downtown Welcome.

"The Cadillac." It was currently parked in Clara's garage, collecting dust.

As much as she loved the idea of the handoffs, she'd stalled planning her trip to California. I hadn't asked her why. I didn't need to.

Returning to California would bring back a barrage of emotions, and she was psyching herself up for it.

"Tomorrow you'll be on your own," Brody said. "Today, I wanted to come along and make the introductions."

"Thank you." It had been nice to have him at my side,

to not do this alone. And though we were still adjusting to sharing a roof, I wouldn't have wanted anyone else at my side, not even Clara. Brody's confidence was contagious, and it had given me that extra boost to dive in. "I think this is a record, Carmichael. We've managed to get along for nearly two days."

"Give it time. I'm sure you'll do something soon to piss me off."

I fought a smile. "Count on it."

Brody rolled down the road, taking every block deliberately, like he was giving me time to inspect each and every storefront.

The coffee shop three doors down from Welcome Floral had green metal tables on the sidewalk and a chalk sandwich board that boasted the daily latte special. An attorney's office had silver letters stenciled on a large plateglass window. Brian's Pub had an orange neon sign that glowed even in broad daylight.

The black streetlamps stood tall, hoisting their clear glass globes. The brick storefronts alternated in shades of classic burnt red and limestone cream. They reminded me of the desert rocks along Route 66, faded and worn but unique.

"It's real here," I said. "Every street."

"Refreshing, isn't it?"

"In Heron Beach, the local neighborhoods were real. You could count on your neighbor for more than just a cup of sugar. But everyone catered to the tourists. You wore a smile at all times. You put on your best show. I never minded because I genuinely enjoyed what I was doing. It's easy to smile when you like your job. But I always made sure to wash my hands before going inside the hotel and clean dirt from my cuticles. I'd tuck in my T-shirt and wipe clean my shoes. I won't have to do that here."

"No. What matters here is who you are."

"Then why do you dress in a suit every day?" I shifted in my seat for a better view of his face. I'd always wanted to know why he dressed so impeccably, especially after seeing him in jeans on Saturday. The image of those long legs in denim was as fresh as the mental picture of him at the gym this morning.

They'd been nice jeans, more expensive than any pair I'd owned in my lifetime, but they'd fit Brody so perfectly. Loose, but not baggy. Fitted, but not tight. They'd showcased his strong thighs and narrow waist.

Unbuttoned, the man was irresistible. If he had leaned in the other night at the pool, I probably would have kissed him.

"I have a meeting with my grandmother," he said.

"Oh, is she here? Because if she is, I'm going to hide at Clara's."

Brody chuckled. "No, she's in Vegas. The meeting is virtual."

"Oh. Do you have meetings with her every day?" It wouldn't surprise me at all if Coreen required he be in a suit.

"Not daily, but often enough."

"But you still wear a suit every day."

"This is really bugging you, isn't it?" The corner of his mouth turned up. "My suits?"

Yes, it was. Because when it came to Brody Carmichael, my curiosity was piqued. "Humor me."

"It's something I started doing years ago. Any day that I'm working, I wear a suit. And I work every day. People expect a certain image from their leader."

"Not Clara. You don't need to dress up for her."

"Yes, I do. She deserves me at my best. All of my employees do. It was something my grandfather always did. He wore a suit every day. He showed up for his company every day."

"And you're showing up too." I took in his handsome profile and the strong cut of his jaw. "You wore jeans on Saturday."

"That was different."

"Why?" Because we were hauling boxes?

"Because that was for you."

One sentence. One answer.

And the world fell away from my feet.

Did he realize what he'd just confessed? Did he realize how special he'd just made me feel?

I was the exception to his rules.

One sentence, one answer, and we were back to that night. He was in a tux. I was in a green gown. And electricity sparked between us.

Brody's hands tightened on the wheel as he picked up speed, racing down the highway toward his house.

Maybe he hadn't meant to let it slip, but it was too late. It was out there, living and breathing and changing everything.

What did this mean? Did he want a relationship? Did I?

I'd been so absorbed in this pregnancy, I hadn't let myself consider my feelings for Brody. I hadn't realized until just this moment that there were even feelings there.

Feelings more than the obvious sexual attraction, because Brody was gorgeous, and I wasn't blind. I *liked* the man behind the suit. I *liked* the man who showed up for his people every day. I *liked* the man who let down his guard just for me.

God, this was so messed up. Any other guy and we'd date. Any other guy and we'd have sex and fun and see if this was the lasting sort of fling.

The baby changed everything.

My mind spun as fast as the Jaguar's wheels. When Brody slowed to open the gate and ease down the drive-way, I still hadn't figured out what to say, probably because I didn't know him. I was walking on eggshells around Brody because he was practically a stranger.

And that was a problem we were going to fix.

"Would you make me a deal?" I asked.

"Depends on the deal." He kept his eyes focused on the road. His spine was ramrod straight. He'd shown me a hint of vulnerability and now he was erecting those walls.

"Have dinner with me. Every night."

"Why?"

"We should know each other. I'd like to know you, Brody."

He glanced over, and in those green eyes, I could so easily lose myself. Brody gave me a single nod, then returned his gaze to the road.

"Thank—" My mouth closed at the black SUV parked in front of the house. "Company?"

He shook his head and parked the car in the driveway.

Ron, who I was convinced had magical powers, appeared out of nowhere to open my door. "Miss Aria."

"Don't bow." I got out and shook my head. "Ron, if we're going to get along, you have to stop bowing like I'm Queen Elizabeth."

The corner of his mouth turned up. Then the wiseass bowed. "Very well, miss."

"You're as insufferable as that one." I hooked a thumb toward Brody.

Ron retrieved a set of keys from his pocket and took them to Brody. Then with a nod, he disappeared inside the house.

"Here." Brody walked over and took my hand in his, pressing the cold metal keys into my palm. "For you."

"For me what?" I jiggled the keys.

"The car. It's for you."

My jaw dropped. "You bought me a car. A BMW. Without asking me about it first."

"Yes. Is that a problem?"

And just like that, our two-day no-fighting streak came to an end.

CHAPTER ELEVEN

BRODY

Her laughter greeted me when the flower shop's door chime faded. I followed the musical sound toward the back of the shop, expecting to find her at the long wooden counter that held the cash register and a fresh bundle of blue hydrangeas. The only reason I knew they were hydrangeas was because of the little chalkboard sign beside it.

Hydrangeas $15/Bunch

There was a metal bell beside the mason jar of pens, and I tapped the plunger, then held my breath.

Marty came out first. The smile on his face dropped, something I'd never seen before because the guy always had a smile for me. "If you're not here to grovel, I'd head to the door before she sees you."

"I'm here to grovel."

"Good." He nodded. "Head on back."

"Thanks." I rounded the counter for the door, ducking into the workroom.

Aria's smile, like Marty's, dropped when she looked past the arrangement she was making. "Are you here to buy me a pony? An island? An island of ponies?"

"Not today."

She picked up a rose from the metal table and stabbed it into the vase she was filling. Her hair was braided over one shoulder with wisps loose around her ears. Her brown eyes sparkled—angry, but I did love their fire. Her cheeks held a pink flush.

Aria was more beautiful than any flower in the world. Even mad, she was lovelier than any rose.

This was the first time I'd seen her in three days, other than small glimpses of her coming and going from Clara's place or this shop. I took her in like a thirsty man standing before a clear mountain stream.

Three days. I'd finally cracked, said to hell with my pride and driven to the flower shop for just one drink.

Aria looked at ease and comfortable here. This was her domain. In just days, she'd made it her own. When I walked into a room, I could usually tell who was in charge. Last month, the shop had been run by Marty. Aria held the power now. And Christ, it was sexy as fuck.

She ignored me and kept working on the arrangement.

Plastic industrial buckets dotted the floor. Some had flowers. Most held discarded stems and leaves. The walls were lined with shelves, each crammed with empty vases in varying shapes and sizes. The long counter that ran the length of the room was littered with scissors and knives and twine and ribbon. Behind Aria, there was an opening to the cool room. The doorway didn't have an actual door, just strips of thick plastic that draped from the frame to the concrete floor.

It was as messy and unorganized as it had been when I'd come down to finalize the purchase with the Backers. We'd sat at that very table, Clara at my side, and signed papers for this shop.

An hour later, while they'd probably been planning their retirement in Hawaii, my lawyer had been busy drawing up a different set of papers. An agreement between Aria and me, one that would ensure she'd never know exactly how much I'd paid for this shop.

"What are you doing here?" She took the scissors in her hand and cut the stem of a rose. The snap rang through the workroom like a sharp bite.

"You've been avoiding me for three days."

"Tell me something I don't know."

I frowned. "I thought you wanted to have dinners together."

"Then you bought me a car without asking."

A car that had been in the exact same place since Monday. The Cadillac, red and gleaming, was what she'd been driving. It was currently parked diagonally on the street outside the shop beside my Jaguar.

Yesterday, I'd asked Clara what it would take to just

buy the Cadillac. She'd informed me that their friend Londyn owned it and Londyn would never sell. *Not everything has a price, Brody.*

The car was a lot like Aria in that regard.

"I wanted you to have a vehicle. Something safe." The BMW I'd bought her came with one of the highest safety ratings available for SUVs.

"People don't just buy other people cars without asking."

"You're right. I should have asked." That way she could have picked the color and style.

"And?" She crossed her arms over her chest.

"And, what?"

Her nostrils flared. "You suck at apologies."

"I'm sorry." I meant it.

"And?"

"And . . . you can have a different car if you want."

Her mouth pursed in a thin line. "And you won't do it again."

"Oh."

"Yeah, oh," she mimicked. "No more buying me stuff."

"Define stuff."

"Anything with a price tag."

I frowned. "That seems extreme."

"You're an extreme sort of man. I trust you can figure this out."

For the sake of ending her cold war, I let it go. Would I stop buying her things? Absolutely not. Especially when the baby came. But for today, I'd change the subject.

I took the envelope from under my arm and set it on the table. "I wanted to bring this by."

"What is it?" She stood, walking closer to flip open the folder.

"It's the deed to the flower shop and the executed contract."

"Oh. Okay." She picked up the papers, running a hand over the first page. "This makes it official."

"It is official."

She stared at the page, not speaking, as a crease formed between her eyebrows.

"What's wrong?"

"I've never owned anything before. Nothing like this." The fear in her voice pierced my heart. "What if I screw it up?"

"You won't." I put a hand on her shoulder, nudging her to turn. When her eyes tipped up to meet mine, the worry in her gaze made it hard to breathe.

She shouldn't worry. She shouldn't have fears. Aria deserved an easy life. I'd make sure of it, if she'd just let me.

"I won't let you fall."

"You say that and it's sweet. But you don't get it."

"Get what?"

"I need to do this on my own."

"Understandable. Think of me as the safety net."

"I've never had a safety net."

"You do now."

Without thinking, I brushed a stray hair away from her temple. One touch and my heart galloped. Aria had said on Monday that she wanted to know me. I wanted to know her too, inside and out. Again and again.

Her eyes searched mine. Her breaths shortened.

It was her lips that drew me in. Before I could rationalize what I was doing, my mouth was on hers and my arms banded around her back.

She let out a small whimper, a mewl, as I dragged my tongue across her lower lip. Then her mouth opened, and I swept inside, savoring the heat of her mouth. Aria gripped the lapels of my jacket, clutching me as her tongue tangled with mine.

Fuck, but she tasted good. Sweet and warm like melted honey.

She molded to my body as I held her close, soaking her in. My pulse pounded and I slid my hands down, fitting my palms to the curve of her ass as I pulled her into my arousal.

Aria moaned, holding me closer, as I swallowed the sound down my throat.

The distant sound of a bell chimed. The front door. The flower shop.

Marty's voice carried to the back room as he greeted the customer. "Hello there. What can I help you with today?"

We snapped to reality and tore our lips apart. Aria blinked rapidly, clearing the fog. I ran a hand over my damp lips.

Then she was gone, stepping away and retreating to the other side of the table. She palmed her forehead, her eyes wide. "That was . . ."

"Sorry."

She waved it off. "It's fine."

Was it fine? Because it felt right. So fucking right. Like we should have been kissing all along. Every day.

"Aria." Marty poked his head around the corner. "Miss Julia from the diner is here. She was hoping to meet you."

"Okay." Aria put on a smile. "Be right there."

"I'll see you at home," I said after Marty disappeared.

Aria nodded, her eyes fixed on a rose. She didn't look up as I turned to leave. The color had drained from her face. Her hand rested on the swell of her belly. She looked . . . petrified.

Damn it.

What the actual fuck had I been thinking?

————

"OH MY GOD." Aria gasped as light flooded the kitchen. Her hand was pressed to her heart. "You scared me."

"Sorry," I said from my seat at the island.

"What are you doing?"

"You asked for dinner together."

"On Monday." She walked into the room, wrapping her arms around her middle. "That was three days ago. And it's nine o'clock."

I shrugged. The stool was hard and my ass had gone numb hours ago. As darkness had settled outside, I hadn't been able to bring myself to move.

"You didn't eat?"

"I was waiting." And thinking. And kicking myself in the ass for kissing her earlier.

Aria's shoulders fell and her arms dropped to her sides. She was wearing a baggy sweatshirt that hit her midthigh. Her toned legs were encased in black leggings. Her feet were bare and her toes painted a sexy hot pink.

Maybe waiting, hoping she'd show, had been a bad idea. I'd wanted to apologize and work this out. But now, seeing her relaxed and at home here, well . . . now I wanted to kiss her again.

"I'm sorry about the kiss," I said. "When it comes to you, I can't seem to help myself."

She padded to the seat beside mine.

I pulled it out for her, waiting until she sat. Then I twisted, leaning an elbow on the counter. I'd discarded my navy pinstripe jacket in my bedroom. I'd rolled up my baby-blue shirtsleeves and undone the top two buttons. Even my tie was gone.

"What are we doing, Brody?" she asked, her voice no louder than a whisper.

"No idea."

"What do you want?"

You. To be a good father. "A healthy baby."

"Then that's our common ground. It has to be our common ground."

I nodded. "Agreed."

"But—"

"Please, don't leave," I blurted. That was all I could think about tonight. That my kiss in the shop earlier would drive her away.

She put her hand on my arm. "I'm not going to leave over a kiss."

The air rushed from my lungs. "Okay."

"I'm starving. I came in to scrounge for a snack." She hopped off her stool and went to the fridge, opening the door. "Did you eat?"

"No."

She glanced over her shoulder. "Because you were waiting."

"I was waiting."

"I'll make us something."

"Ron has leftovers. Enchiladas. Pasta pomodoro. Roasted chicken and vegetables."

"Wow." She whistled. "Go Ron. What do you feel like?"

"Food."

Aria laughed and pulled out the container on the middle shelf. Then she went about warming up our plates.

Enchiladas. When she settled in beside me, we both tore into the meal.

"Didn't you eat dinner?" I asked.

"Yes, I did. But I get hungry at night." She put her hand on her belly. "This kid is going to be a night owl."

"I'm excited," I admitted. "I get more anxious every day to meet him or her. To learn what he or she will be like."

"So do I." Aria's eyes softened. "I'm really excited."

The giddiness on her face was a rush. A comfort. Who else could I share that with but her?

"I haven't told anyone," I admitted. "Except Ron."

"I didn't have many people to tell but Clara and the girls from the junkyard."

"What did they say?"

She smiled. "They're happy for me. Gemma just had a baby. Katherine is pregnant. Londyn has a little girl and a baby too. Clara has August. It's been fun to share this with them. To have that in common."

"I'm glad."

She ate a few bites, then set her fork down. "Why haven't you told anyone?"

I sighed. "Because my family has a way of ruining the good things in my life. I won't let them ruin this."

"That's understandable. I can't see your grandmother doing cartwheels over the fact that this *stray* is pregnant." Aria rolled her eyes. "But eventually, you'll have to tell them."

"Eventually. Like when he or she graduates from high school."

Aria giggled. "Do you want to find out if we're having a boy or a girl?"

"Yes. No. I don't know. Do you?"

"No." She grinned. "I like surprises."

"Then a surprise it is." I nodded and took another bite. "This is good."

"Ron is quite the chef."

"Yes, but that's not what I meant. This, the conversation, is good. I almost enjoy your presence when you're not snapping at me," I teased.

She huffed. "Well, you haven't tried to buy me anything in the past fifteen minutes, so it makes me less snappy."

I chuckled. "Then we'll avoid all discussion of material things."

"Can I ask you something?"

"Of course."

"You rarely talk about your parents. What happened to them? I only ask because I'd like to know. One day, this kid is going to ask the same question. It would be nice to know the answer before then."

"Fair enough." I set my fork down and wiped my mouth with a cloth napkin. "My mother is Coreen's daughter. She got pregnant with me when she was seventeen. Needless to say, that didn't go over well."

Aria cringed. "I can't see your grandmother happy. Ever. But especially with a teen pregnancy."

"Mom didn't go to college like her parents had planned. She didn't go to work for Carmichael Communications like they'd planned. She didn't give me up for adoption like they'd insisted."

"How do you even know that? It seems cruel."

"That's my family." I lifted a shoulder. "My grandfather was brutally forthcoming. When I was ten, he sat me down, and instead of telling me about the birds and the bees, he laid out exactly what my mother had done to disappoint him. And he did it in a way that I knew I had no choice but to fall in line. He assumed the role of my father that day."

"And that didn't bother your dad?"

"No, because my father would never argue or go against Grandfather's wishes. My father married my mother and ditched his own last name for Carmichael. He saw my grandparents as his meal ticket, and if that meant giving up a kid, so be it."

"You were only ten." She gave me a sad smile. "I guess both of our lives changed at ten."

"I guess they did."

"I'm sorry."

"Don't be. I look at Alastair and think I got the better end of the deal. My grandparents, despite all their threats, never cut my mother off. They bought her a house and provided a life for her and my father. Neither of my parents ever had a job. They never had responsibility. They remained teenagers in a sense because my grandparents enabled them. I went to live with my grandparents at ten, Alastair was only five. He stayed with our parents. And they spoiled him rotten."

"That's . . . sad." She scrunched up her nose. "I don't like Alastair and you're making me feel bad for him."

"Don't." I chuckled. "Maybe as a kid he couldn't help himself, but he's an adult and his choices are his own. He's a dick because he wants to be a dick."

"You said it." She picked up her water and raised it to her lips. I stared, blatantly, as she drank, jealous of a glass because it got to touch her mouth. "So you moved in with your grandparents."

"Technically. Though they sent me away to private schools, so I was rarely in their home. Only on school breaks and holidays."

"And your parents? Did you see them?"

"At times. It became harder and harder to be around them as I got older. They were never going to grow up. They were never going to stop spending money and feeding bad habits. Especially Dad."

"What habits?"

"The wrong ones." Drugs. Booze. Women. "My parents died in a car accident."

"You told me."

"Dad was driving. He was high and drunk on their way to a casino. He veered off the road, lost control and slammed their vehicle into a tree going seventy miles per hour."

Aria winced and closed her eyes. "God."

"At least they didn't hit another car." Like a car carrying parents. "That was seven years ago."

"Brody." She stretched her hand out and covered my wrist. "I'm sorry."

I put my palm over her knuckles. "I'm sorry too."

It had taken me a long time not to feel like the cause of my mother's downfall. It had taken me well into adulthood to realize that she'd made her own choices. Still, at a young age, I'd seen the mess that was her life. I'd recognized the difference in my mother's lifestyle compared to mothers of friends from school. And I'd felt responsible. My birth had been the trigger.

But I hadn't been the one holding the gun.

She'd made her choices. She'd died because of them.

"Thank you for telling me," Aria said.

"You're welcome. One day, I'd like to know your story too. If you'll share it with me."

Aria dipped her chin. "I will. But not tonight."

"There's no rush. I'll be here when you're ready." I stood and took our empty dishes to the sink, rinsing them out and putting them in the dishwasher.

When I was done, I turned, just as Aria's gaze flicked up. She'd been staring at my ass. And the lust in her eyes was unmistakable.

"You can't look at me like that," I pleaded.

She swallowed hard. "I can't help it."

I knew the feeling.

My feet carried me across the kitchen, right to her space. I stood above her, staring down into those beautiful brown eyes, and let myself drown.

"I told myself earlier I wasn't going to make this a habit. That I couldn't let you kiss me again." Her hand snaked up my stomach, her palm rising to where my heart was beating out of my chest. "But what if we did?"

A pained groan escaped my throat. "I want you. I fucking crave you, Aria."

She flipped open a button on my shirt. "Then you'd better kiss me again."

CHAPTER TWELVE

ARIA

Holy sweet Jesus, this man could kiss.

Brody swept me off the stool the moment his lips seared mine. The energy, the anticipation, the longing was like climbing to the top of a peak and jumping off into the abyss.

Was this a mistake? Was this reckless? Yes, on both counts, but I wasn't going to stop, and as Brody carried me from the kitchen, I knew he wasn't going to either.

"God, you taste good." He latched on to my pulse, licking and sucking the skin at my throat.

I held on to his shoulders and closed my eyes, savoring the wet heat of his tongue as his strides hastened toward the staircase. Since moving in, I hadn't ventured to the second floor much. I'd done my best not to snoop more than once or twice on his side of the house, deciding it was best to stay away from that invisible boundary.

Brody crashed right through it and, much like the night of the wedding, carried me toward his bedroom.

His hands held me tight with a grip under my ass. He peppered my jaw with a trail of kisses before breaking away to climb the steps. His green eyes were dark with hunger. His face was like granite, nearly unreadable. Except I'd seen this look before. The last time he'd carted me to his bed.

This was Brody on a mission. He was all business. Serious. Stoic. I grinned, because I also knew how quickly he'd flip the switch and become the sensual lover. Last time, it had happened before my dress had pooled to the floor.

Brody took the stairs two at a time, even with my legs wrapped tightly around his hips.

My chest heaved as I tried to regain my breath. The heat between us was like standing in the middle of an active volcano.

We reached the landing and Brody jostled me, hoisting me higher so that my center pressed against his zipper. A whimper escaped my throat. My core was drenched and aching. The throb in my body vibrated from my bones, shaking me from skull to toe.

Brody stormed through his open bedroom door, then he had me on the bed, setting me down and covering me with his weight. His lips slammed down on mine, his tongue plunging deep.

I moaned and threaded my fingers through his hair,

letting the short strands at the nape tickle my palms. The longer strands were like silk against my fingertips as Brody ravaged my mouth, exploring every corner.

When had a kiss been so erotic? Not even the night of the wedding had I been this close to an orgasm from a kiss alone. Thank you, hormones.

I spread my legs, making room to cradle Brody's hips with mine. The steel rod behind his slacks rubbed against the thin fabric of my leggings.

"Yes," I moaned when he rocked against me, his lips trailing down my throat.

He found my pulse again and sucked. "I want to taste you."

I gulped. "Yes."

His hands dove under the hem of my sweatshirt, sliding up my ribs. When he found that I wasn't wearing a bra, his entire body froze. Those green eyes whipped to mine.

"Spoiler alert." I winked. "I'm not wearing panties either."

A slow grin spread across his face as he pulled away and stood from the bed. "Next time don't tell me. I like surprises too."

Next time.

I wanted a next time. We hadn't even gotten to the good stuff tonight and I was already looking forward to doing it again.

And again.

And again.

Brody's long fingers slipped into the waistband of my leggings. He tugged, stripping them over my hips. When my bare mound came into view, his eyes flared, and he ran his tongue over his bottom lip. *Ravenous.* He was ravenous for me.

I squirmed, hoping he'd ditch the leggings and get down to business. But he took his time, pulling them inch by inch, collecting the stretchy cotton in his hands as he worked lower and lower.

Finally, he pulled them off my feet and tossed them over a shoulder.

"Christ, you're beautiful." He knelt at the foot of the bed, hooking his hands behind my knees. Then with a fast tug, he had me splayed before him.

Brody didn't linger. He dove in, flattening his tongue as he tasted my glistening folds. When he reached my clit, I nearly came off the bed.

"Oh my God." I writhed, shaking and trembling for more.

He licked me again. "You taste fucking incredible."

My hands found their way into his hair, gripping it as he feasted. The torture was pure ecstasy and I succumbed to the build. It came in a rush, hard and fast. My toes curled as the sensation swallowed me whole and I orgasmed on Brody's lips, moaning his name and praising the angel who'd blessed him with such a gifted tongue.

The aftershocks shook my limbs as he stood but the

sound of his belt buckle loosening snapped me out of my sated stupor. I cracked my eyes open and propped up on an elbow as he worked the buttons on his shirt with practiced efficiency. He tugged it free from his slacks and whipped it off his arms.

Brody's body was mouthwatering. I hadn't appreciated it enough the night of the wedding. His stomach was made of perfect squares, the definition between them crisp and lickable. His arms were honed to perfection, muscle upon muscle. The veins beneath his skin bulged. I'd be tracing those little lines later with my tongue.

My eyes drifted lower, taking his body in with a slow perusal.

"Sweatshirt." He jerked his chin. "Off."

I sat up and stripped it as fast as I could, not wanting to miss the show as he shoved down his pants and the white boxer briefs beneath. They slid off his thick legs, the muscles as defined on his lower half as they were the top. I'd study them later because right now, my gaze was fixed on his swollen cock. The velvet shaft was hard and long, the tip decorated with a pearled drop.

Brody came into the bed, taking me deeper into the pillows. Then he dropped his mouth to my throat, his breath fluttering there before he took a deep inhale.

"You smell like flowers."

I hummed, closing my eyes as the heat from his bare skin warmed mine. Brody smelled like spice and earth. It was a clean scent, rich and robust, like the man himself. A scent I missed when I went too long without a pull.

He was an addiction. I'd had no trouble giving up wine or lunch meat or soft cheese during this pregnancy. But if someone asked me to give up Brody's scent, I wouldn't be able to do it.

In all these months, I hadn't let myself believe that the night of the wedding had been anything more than sex. A one-night stand. Except it had meant more, hadn't it? Not just because of the baby, but because Brody was . . . special. Lasting.

"Will this be okay?" He leaned back with concern in his eyes. "Sex?"

"For the baby?"

He nodded.

"It's fine." I wrapped my legs around his ass, raising my hips to brush my soaking center against his erection.

Brody hissed, his jaw flexing as he closed his eyes. "If I hurt you—"

"You won't." I urged him closer. "Come inside."

That sharp jaw flexed again, like he was fighting for control, then he positioned himself at my entrance and slid deep.

My breath hitched when the root of his cock pressed against my clit. My back arched off the plush bed and my fingertips dug into the skin at his shoulders.

"Fuck, you feel good." He dropped a line of open-mouthed kisses across my chest, right along the swell of my breasts. "So good."

"Move." I gripped his arms, holding tight as he slid out and rocked us together again.

The night of the wedding, he'd fucked me. Hard. The next morning my core had ached from the power of his thrusts. But tonight would be different. We both needed it easy. With the baby, this wasn't a rough and rowdy tumble in his sheets. This was the slow savor. The steady climb.

Stroke after stroke, Brody glided us together. He never gave me all his weight, careful to hover above my body. His thrusts were full of the same grace he held in every movement. The roll of his hips. The firm press.

My God, he knew how to give pleasure. My breaths turned to pants. My toes dug into the comforter. My hands gripped its gray cotton, squeezing it as my inner walls fluttered around Brody.

"Aria," he whispered into my ear. One of his hands dropped to mine, threading his fingers between mine and raising it above my head. He pinned it to the headboard, then did the same with the other.

"You're so tight. So wet." His hands held my arms there, his fingers tight to mine. "Come, baby. Come for me. Come while I fuck you."

The naughty words shot straight to my pussy and I exploded, crying his name as I lost control. White spots exploded in my vision. My legs shook and my arms, still locked above my head, pulled hard against Brody's locked grip. Through my release, his hips never slowed, and when I dared open my eyes and return to earth, his green gaze was waiting.

"That was . . ." Brody's throat bobbed. "Beautiful. God, you are beautiful."

I tipped my hips, drawing him deeper into my body. "Your turn."

He moved, faster and faster, still using care. Then his lips crashed down on mine, my taste lingering on his tongue, and he kissed me until his release came over him and he poured himself into my body.

"Fuck," he groaned, dropping his forehead to mine as he came down from the rush. Then he twisted, rolling to his back and taking me with him.

I collapsed on his chest, struggling to regain my breath.

A lock of hair was in my face but my arms were too weak to push it away. I huffed a breath, trying to blow it free. When that didn't work, Brody tucked it behind an ear for me.

"Should we talk about this?" he asked.

I shook my head. "No. We should sleep."

Tomorrow there would be time to talk. Tonight, I only wanted to rest.

And not think about the fact that we might have just ruined everything.

———

"OH MY GOD."

The words woke me from a dreamless sleep.

I sat up, remembering just in time that I was naked in Brody's bedroom. I clutched the sheet to my chest and blinked the fog from my eyes. Then I squinted at my sister, who stood in the doorway to Brody's bedroom.

"Clara?" My voice was groggy and my head fuzzy. I glanced at the clock on the nightstand, doing a double take at the time. *Eight thirteen.* When was the last time I'd slept past five?

"I was just looking for Brody." Her eyes stayed fixed on the floor. "We always meet at eight. I didn't see him in the office and the door was open so . . ."

Beside me, Brody stirred. "Bump it to nine."

"Okay." She spun around too fast, nearly colliding with the doorframe as she scurried down the hall.

I fell back onto a pillow. Brody's was the most comfortable bed I'd slept on in my life. Maybe that was why my internal alarm clock had taken the day off, even though I couldn't.

I was due at the flower shop to meet Marty when it opened at ten. It was taking some getting used to, not arriving at work before dawn. The hours would get longer as I learned more, but for the first week, I was easing into my new routine.

Today, he was introducing me to the bookkeeper who'd come on to do the accounting after Brody had purchased the shop. Then we were going to do a walk-through of the store and prioritize redecoration.

But first . . . there was a man in my bed.

Or I was in his.

"Now should we talk about this?" Brody asked. His eyes were still closed, and he was hugging his pillow. The sheet had fallen low, nearly to his ass, and the strong, wide plane of his back was on full display.

The responsible decision would be to discuss this and agree on how sex would or would not fit into our relationship.

"No." I whipped the covers off and kicked my legs over the bed. Then I stood, hurrying to tug on my sweatshirt and pull on my leggings. "Later. I need to get ready for work."

And I needed to think this through.

Without another word, I tucked my bedhead hair behind my ears and aimed my feet at the door.

"Aria." Brody's voice stopped me before I could disappear.

"Yeah?" I turned.

He'd sat up. His hair was mussed, his face sleepy. But his eyes were alert and commanding. "See you at dinner."

I nodded, then ran.

By a miracle, I managed to avoid Ron when I walked through the kitchen but the smell of bacon told me he was close. Escaping to my side of the house, I thought I was home-free when my bedroom door came into view—until I walked in and found my sister sitting on the bed with a smirk on her pretty face.

My face flushed and I kicked the door closed behind me. "Don't look at me like that."

She raised an eyebrow. "Like what?"

"You're all . . . smug."

"I'm not smug."

"Then you need a mirror." I walked to the bed, plopping down beside her. Then I covered my face in my hands. "This is a disaster."

She giggled. "Dramatic much?"

"I had sex with Brody."

"Duh. You're pregnant."

"Last night, Clara."

"I'll repeat. Duh."

I swatted at her as she laughed. "You're not helping."

"What do you want me to say? I love you. I love Brody. When you two are in the same room, the sexual tension is so thick I've nearly choked on it for the past ten years."

"What?" I sat up. "Nu-uh."

"Please." She rolled her eyes. "It was only a matter of time before you realized you don't really hate him the way you want to hate him."

I frowned. "You're a pain in my ass."

"And you love me too. This could be a good thing. You're having a baby."

"Exactly!" I threw my hands in the air. "What if we

try this and fail? What if we truly end up hating one another? I don't want my child in the middle of that."

"But what if it works? What if . . . what if you can give your child the life that I can never give August?"

My heart twisted. "Clara, you're a good mom. The best."

"And you will be too. Even if it doesn't work, Brody is a good man. You can navigate this."

I blew out a deep breath, leaning into her side. "I don't know what I'm doing. With men. I haven't had many in my life. And any guy I've slept with was a guy I dated. Brody was my first hookup."

There were reasons why I was so selective when it came to lovers. Reasons why I was careful with who I let touch my body. Reasons I wouldn't let myself think of today or talk about with Clara.

I wouldn't drag her back to that place.

Four lovers. That was the extent of my experience. My first had been a man I'd dated in Vegas. He'd taken me on eight dates before I'd given him my virginity. I'd dumped him before date number nine because I'd been so mortified by my fears during sex.

As different boyfriends had come and gone, I'd worked through many of those fears, but they still lingered. It was difficult for me to give up control of my body. To surrender it to a man.

Until Brody.

Brody beat back the anxiety when it came to sex. There

were no insecurities with him. He made it easy to relax and enjoy. Maybe because he oozed confidence and authority. Every touch was deliberate. Every caress solid. There was no fumbling, and in that surety, he made me feel safe.

Last night, and the night of the wedding, he'd given me everything I'd needed to shut out the noise and just . . . be.

"He's not who I thought he was," I whispered. Beneath the cement and glass exterior, there was a big, beating, beautiful heart. "What would you do?"

"Trust him," she answered without hesitation. "Give him time. He's learning too."

Trust him. At least Brody had always been honest with me. There were no secrets. No lies.

I could trust him.

Clara and I sat together in silence until she had to go meet Brody for her meeting and I had to shower before going to the shop.

I drove the Cadillac into town, not ready yet to concede that the BMW Brody had bought was a really nice car. After a fun day with Marty, soaking in his wisdom and imparting some of my own, I returned home.

It hadn't been easy to ignore thoughts of Brody at work, but I'd tried. When I walked in the house and his smell hit my nose, I knew with one breath I was in trouble.

So instead of meeting him for dinner like he'd expected, I stayed in my bedroom, watching the clock tick away until dinner. My stomach growled but I didn't move. Cowardice was a different look for me and one I suspected wasn't all that becoming.

What did I say? Did I want a relationship? Did I have the energy to nourish this baby and give attention to anyone else? What if Brody thought it best we return to platonic cohabitation?

The last question scared me the most.

Because it would hurt. More than I wanted to admit. If Brody rejected me, that was going to freaking sting.

An hour passed as I lay on my bed, my eyes trained on the ceiling as the anxieties flourished like a freshly watered tulip. The sun was setting outside, casting the pool with its glow.

Shifting one ear into a pillow, I studied the colors as they faded. Blue to yellow. Yellow to orange. Pink to red. I did love desert sunsets. Bright and beautiful, I found myself on the back patio often, watching the colors shift over the dusty horizon.

In the mornings, I'd venture outside to watch the desert bloom. Years of visiting Clara and I hadn't timed a trip in the early spring, probably because March was always a hectic time at The Gallaway, planting for the season. Boy, had I missed out.

It was just beginning, but soon, the wildflower super bloom would carpet the rugged landscapes in pinks and yellows and purples. Clara had told me it was beautiful, but even now, at the beginning, words hadn't done the spectacle justice.

The spring desert was truly breathtaking, and it was only the start.

When I'd stopped wanting to hate it here, I'd fallen in love.

"You missed dinner."

I flinched, sitting up with a jolt.

Brody stood in the doorway with one ankle crossed over the other. His feet were bare, his jacket and tie gone. His shirtsleeves were rolled up and the buttons at his throat were undone. Just like last night. And just like last night, I couldn't take my eyes off him.

"I wasn't sure if dinner was a good idea," I confessed. "I wasn't sure what to say."

He pushed off the door and walked into the room. Then he climbed on the bed, lying at my side. "I'm not sure what to say either."

"Really?" I propped up on an elbow. "You always seem sure."

"Not always. Do we have to decide now?"

Clara's advice had been to give him time. And here he was, asking for it too.

So instead of worrying, I leaned closer and brushed his lips with mine.

"No. I guess we don't."

CHAPTER THIRTEEN

BRODY

"I have to go." I kissed Aria's bare shoulder as she combed her wet hair. She wore the towel she'd wrapped around her body after her shower. A shower I'd missed because I'd been in my own bathroom preparing for what would likely be an exhausting day.

"Have a safe trip."

"I will." I kissed her shoulder again, then took a long look at her in the mirror.

My God, she was gorgeous. If we had a girl, I hoped she looked exactly like Aria. If we had a boy, I wanted him to have her bewitching eyes.

"I think I'll tell her."

The comb in Aria's hand froze. "Are you sure?"

"Would you mind?"

She shook her head. "We can't keep this a secret forever."

"All right. Then I'll do it today." It would be better to tell Grandmother about the baby in person.

I was flying to Vegas today for a string of meetings, but I had an hour carved out after lunch to catch up with Grandmother. She wasn't going to like this—the baby or Aria—and I didn't give a single fuck.

This was my child and I was excited. The fear of fatherhood was there, a constant worry at the back of my mind, and I suspected it'd be there for the remainder of my life. But excitement had taken center stage, especially now that Aria and I had started . . .

Sleeping together? Dating? I hadn't dated since college. Since Aria and I rarely went anywhere outside the home, I doubted this would qualify.

Maybe I should change that.

"Tomorrow night, I'd like to take you out to dinner."

Aria returned to her brushing. "Okay. I've been craving a burger from the diner ever since Marty and I ordered in lunch from there last week."

"The diner it is." I drew a circle on her shoulder with my finger, then reluctantly stepped away. It was nearly impossible to keep my hands to myself when she was within reach. And if I kept touching her, that towel would hit the floor and I'd be late for my flight.

"Don't work too hard. No lifting heavy arrangements."

"Yes, sir." A smile toyed at her mouth.

She'd started teasing me lately, calling me sir. The three-letter word sent a rush of heat to my groin.

"You're evil." I didn't hide the adjustment I made to my hardening dick.

Her smile widened. "I know."

I chuckled and walked out of the bathroom while I still could, then headed to the garage. I pulled off the property and onto the highway. Within a mile, I missed home. I missed her.

I wasn't exactly a homebody. Clara called me an introvert, but mostly, I didn't like many people. Many people didn't like me. With so much work to be done, why make friends when I didn't have time to give them? Why date a woman who would only demand attention I didn't have to spare?

Aria was the exception.

When it came to her, none of my rules applied. She had my focus. She had my free moments. She had my nights.

It had been two weeks since the night Aria had told me to kiss her in the kitchen. Two weeks and we hadn't spent a night apart. There were some evenings when I had to work late and I'd find her in her room, tucked into bed, reading a book. Other nights, we'd eat dinner together before I'd start the process of giving her as many orgasms as I could until she passed out.

Those were the best nights.

We slept in her room. My room. Wherever we landed. And never had my house felt so much like a home.

She'd bring home flowers from the shop. They'd sit on

the kitchen counter, brightening it for the weekend. The arrangement she'd brought five days ago had started to droop and I suspected there'd be a new one tonight when I got home from Vegas.

My flight left on time. My morning meetings went off without a hitch. And when it was time to meet with Grandmother and tell her the news, her initial reaction was exactly as I'd expected. A double blink. A demand to repeat myself. Then the fury set in.

"How could you be so foolish?" she snapped, her face as red as I'd seen in a year.

"It wasn't intentional."

"Maybe for you. That woman is trash. She did this on purpose."

"I can assure you, Aria was just as surprised as I was."

"Then she should be an actress." Grandmother scoffed. "Because that woman only wants your money."

If she only knew how wrong she was. Aria still hadn't so much as touched the keys for the BMW I'd bought her. She'd made her first monthly payment on the flower shop even when I'd tried once more to tell her it was unnecessary. Three days ago, I'd heard her tell Ron that whether he liked it or not, she was picking up some groceries on the way home. He was smarter than I was and chose not to argue and had reluctantly handed over his list.

"Whether you like her or not, Aria is in my life," I said. "I won't forsake my child. Or my child's mother."

"Then you prove my point. You were an easy target."

I pinched the bridge of my nose. "Please. Can you just be happy for me? I want this."

"Then you're as foolish as your mother."

My jaw clenched. "I guess I am."

"You will get a nanny. You will find someone suitable to raise that baby so he doesn't turn out like his mother."

"I have a nanny." I sighed.

Or I would have a nanny. Ron had already begun lining up interviews. We'd likely hire someone outside of Welcome, meaning we'd build another home on the property. There was time.

"Unbelievable." Grandmother sat rigid behind her desk, her entire frame locked tight.

"Aria is a kind, loving person. I realize you two didn't start off on the right foot. Ironically, she has as much tenacity as you. If you give her a chance, I'm sure you'll get along."

"She is trash, Broderick. Trash." She made the statement sound like fact. *The sky is blue. The oceans are deep. She is trash.*

Except Aria Saint-James was not trash.

Nothing I said would convince Grandmother otherwise, so why was I here wasting my breath on a woman who was never going to change her mind?

I wouldn't let her steal this joy.

"We're done here." I stood from the chair and walked to the door.

"Get back here. Immediately. I am not done speaking."

I kept walking.

"Broderick."

Aria had been right. My full name really was pretentious. Grandmother knew I preferred Brody.

"Broderick! I will sell this company. If you don't deal with this woman and find a way to get her out of our lives, I will sell this company."

I stopped walking and turned. "Aria is the mother of my child. She is in our lives whether you like it or not."

"Get rid of her. Pay her to disappear."

"No."

"Don't push me. I will sell."

"No, you won't." For too long, she'd made that threat.

It was time to call her bluff.

"You won't sell this company. You won't sell Grandfather's legacy. And you won't threaten me with it again. This is *my* company."

"Not yet, it isn't. I'll sell."

"You can make that decision, but I truly hope you don't. I hope you care about me and my future enough to give me the opportunity to prove myself."

A flicker of guilt crossed her gaze.

Grandfather had stipulated she receive a monthly stipend as the executor of my trust. Knowing him, it had been a heavy sum, enough to tie her to his company. And she'd also receive a sum when her time as trustee ran out. Maybe he'd worried that she'd sell after his death.

I'd assumed that she didn't need the stipend. And that if she sold, she'd receive more money for her own shares than the stipend and lump sum together. But maybe Grandmother's personal finances weren't as strong as they once were. Or maybe the offers for Carmichael that she'd bragged about had been greatly exaggerated.

Whatever her motives, I wasn't going to stick around and listen to her shred Aria.

"Have a nice day, Grandmother."

"Broderick."

"I'm sure we'll talk soon."

"Broderick!"

Grandmother was still yelling as I shoved open the door and disappeared to my own office. I slammed the door shut and went to the windows overlooking the city.

God, she made life difficult. After my birthday, after she was out of Carmichael, I suspected Grandmother would mostly disappear from my life.

I just had to endure until my birthday.

What if I didn't?

What if I walked away? What if I let it all go? The years and years of work I'd put into this place. Was it even worth it?

Yes. My vision was worth fighting for. So were the employees.

I could lead them and this company into a bright

future. Just yesterday, I'd had a call with the CEO of a large communications corporation in California. It had been a casual visit, but we'd danced around a potential deal in the future.

So I'd deal with Grandmother's dramatics and barked orders. I'd do it for employees like Erika, the head of human resources, who'd been working at Carmichael for twenty-eight years. She was eighteen months from retirement, and if the company dissolved before then, she'd lose the twenty-five-thousand-dollar bonus Grandfather had set up for employees who'd worked here for thirty years. That bonus meant Erika could move to Idaho and live closer to her son and grandkids.

I'd endure for Joshua, the head of security who'd started here as a custodian. He was a single father whose daughter was in college. He was determined to pay for her education and his job was the key to that dream.

I would deal with Grandmother for Matt because that poor guy was her third personal assistant this year. He'd just graduated from college and this was his first job. I'd asked him once, after witnessing Grandmother tear into him for getting her coffee order wrong, why he wanted to work at Carmichael. He'd told me his young wife was undergoing chemotherapy and no other job he could find offered such comprehensive health insurance.

Erika, Joshua, Matt. They were all trapped in their jobs.

And I'd stay trapped in mine.

"Brody?" A knock came at the door and I turned from the window as Laney, my second assistant, walked into the room with a stack of papers in her hand. "Your two o'clock is early. Would you like me to show him to a conference room to wait? Or would you like to get started early?"

"I'm ready. Send him in. And let's see if we can move up or cancel my last meeting. I'd like to get home before dark."

"Of course." She smiled, more brightly than normal. Probably because I'd told her this morning that I was going to be a father. She'd been especially smiley since.

I wasn't close to Laney like I was Clara. She lived in Vegas, so we didn't see each other as often. I'd never consider her a personal friend, but she was a nice woman and a fantastic employee. She had two young kids who attended our onsite daycare for employees.

The remainder of my meetings went quickly, and I was able to get out of Vegas an hour earlier than planned. When the plane's wheels touched down in Welcome, I breathed and unknotted my tie.

I'd stripped it off completely, along with my jacket, by the time I parked in the garage at home. Ready for dinner and a long night worshiping Aria's body, I opened the door to a loud crash.

"Aria." I ran toward the source of the noise.

Another crash. "Shit."

"Aria!" A cold gust of air hit me as I rounded the corner and rushed toward her bedroom.

The patio doors were open. Beyond them, the pool shimmered in the March evening light. The sunsets had been beautiful, and two nights ago, Aria had insisted on sitting out by the pool, bundled in a sweater and wool socks, to watch the colorful show.

Her room was cold and empty. I checked the bathroom, where I'd left her this morning, but it was dark. Another crash echoed from the hallway and I jogged to the room next door.

And there she was, standing in the middle of a mess. Boxes were strewn across the floor. A crate had been ripped open with the hammer and pry bar clutched in her hands. The crate's paper stuffing had exploded through the room.

"What's going on?"

Aria whirled, the hand with the hammer ready to strike. "Don't sneak up on me."

"I called for you." I walked into the room as her arm dropped to her side. But the look of fury on her face didn't fade.

"You ordered a cradle?" She pointed the tool at the crate where the soft wooden edge of the cradle peeked out from the packing paper straws.

"Yes."

"And what's in that one?" She glared at the crate in the corner.

"A rocking chair."

Aria's nostrils flared. "You didn't think I'd want to have some input?"

"No." *Shit.* "I figured if you didn't like them, we could send them back and get something else."

"When did you order them?"

"Months ago. They were both custom-made and I knew it would take time."

She crossed her arms, her grip on both tools tightening. "And what about the nanny? I got home from work and Ron was escorting his top candidate out. He wanted to make sure I could meet her before he gave you the final recommendation."

My stomach dropped. This wasn't about the cradle or the chair. This was about the nanny. "It's just an idea."

"A nanny? You think I want a nanny?"

"Well . . . yes."

She threw the tools to the floor of the crate with a clank and thud. "Stop doing this."

"I'm trying to help."

"You're not helping!" The flush rose in her cheeks.

"Aria, this isn't a big deal. Calm down."

"Calm down? No. And this is a big deal." She shook her head. "First it's the car. Then it's the cradle. Then it's the nanny. You make these decisions, these important decisions, without talking to me."

Christ. "I'm sorry."

"Then stop doing it." Her shoulders fell. "Don't make decisions *for* me. Ask me. Share with me. Talk to me."

"Like you talk to me?"

"I talk to you." She planted her hands on her hips. It was then that I noticed her feet were bare amidst wood splinters and metal staples.

I shook my head and turned, stalking away. Knowing she'd follow because Aria didn't let battles go unfought.

She caught up to me in my bedroom, where I was stowing my cufflinks.

"What was that supposed to mean?" she snapped.

I didn't answer.

Instead, I went to work on my shirt's buttons, stripping it off and tossing it in the hamper. Then I pulled a black T-shirt from a drawer and tugged it on. My slacks got traded for the jeans Aria loved so much. And I put on some tennis shoes so I could wade into the mess she'd made in the nursery because she was pissed.

Well, I was pissed too. More than I'd realized.

I was trying to help. Maybe I'd fucked it up. I should have told her about the nanny but I hadn't expected Ron to work so quickly. I certainly hadn't expected him to have an interviewee here at the house.

Why couldn't Aria give me a little credit? And a little slack? I was trying to make her life easier. Why wouldn't she let me?

None of those thoughts were voiced. They stayed trapped in my head as I stalked back to the nursery.

Aria followed, silently fuming. She leaned against the doorjamb as I took the cradle from the box, then unpacked the rocking chair. And once they were out of the way, I went about cleaning up the mess on the floor.

She didn't say a word. Neither did I.

Aria stared. I worked.

Carrying the last piece of the dismantled crates to the garage, I returned to the nursery to find Aria gone. Along with the cradle.

"Damn it, woman." I marched out of the nursery and to her bedroom.

She'd dragged the cradle to the foot of the bed where she sat, rocking it gently.

The cradle was wooden with sleek lines, simple but stylish. I thought she'd be proud that I'd picked something in a warm shade, especially when white and gray had been options.

"This is pretty," she whispered.

"If you want something else, we can get something else."

She shook her head and looked up to meet my gaze. All of the anger she'd been wearing earlier had disappeared. Somewhere during my trips to and from the garage, the fight had gone out of her.

I realized as I crossed the room to sit beside her that my anger had deflated too. "I'm sorry. I said it earlier. I meant it."

"I know. You don't say things you don't mean." She leaned into my side, her hair tickling my bare forearm. "I don't want a nanny. I want to be the one to change diapers and puree baby food and get up in the middle of the night."

"Are you sure?"

She nodded. "No nanny. I'm going to be selfish and keep all of my baby's moments for myself."

"Just share some with me, okay?"

"You can have the poopy diapers."

I chuckled. "So generous."

"And I want a will. I want one ready the day he or she is born. If something happens to us, no matter what, Clara gets custody."

My insides clenched. Just the idea that she—we—might not be there to see our child grow up made me sick. But Aria was right. This was important. "I'll have my attorney draft it up tomorrow."

She sat statue still, staring at the crib with her temple on my shoulder. "My parents didn't have a will. To this day, it's the one thing I haven't been able to forgive them for. It wouldn't have taken more than an hour or two. A phone call to a lawyer. But they put it off and then . . . they were gone."

"We'll have one," I promised, then did my best not to tense because I didn't want her to stop talking.

I knew only pieces of her history, the parts Clara had trusted me with over the years. But I wanted the full story and I wanted it from Aria. I wanted her to trust me with her past, like I'd trusted her with mine.

"Since they didn't have a will, Clara and I became

wards of the state while their estate was settled. We spent four weeks in foster care, waiting for family services to sort out where to stick us."

"You ended up with an uncle, right?"

"Uncle Craig." She shivered. "My mom's stepbrother. They were estranged. My grandmother had been a single mom. She'd had Mom young. Then later she'd remarried a man a few years older, with a son. Her husband died but my grandma kept Craig. It was his senior year, I think. I didn't know my grandma well. She died when Clara and I were babies. My dad's parents were living in a retirement village outside of Phoenix, of all places. Not that far from here."

"And you didn't go with them?"

She shook her head. "I'm sure that's what Mom and Dad had expected to happen. But when my uncle offered to take us, family services thought it was for the best. He was younger and lived in Temecula too, so we wouldn't have to move to a different town. And my dad's parents didn't put up a fight. They didn't want us, not really."

It broke my heart that she'd felt unwanted. That she'd been at the mercy of the adults in her life. I could relate. It had been crushing to feel like a pawn and a burden rather than a child.

"I will never go back to California." Her voice turned cold like the air drifting in from the open patio doors. "Clara wants to go back. She'll take the Cadillac and return because she needs that closure."

"And what do you need?" I'd give it to her. Without question.

"I need that son of a bitch to rot in hell for the rest of eternity."

I twisted, forcing her to sit straight, because I had to see her face. "Did he . . ." I gulped, not even able to choke out the words.

"There was a reason he and my mother were estranged. I'll never know if he did something to her. But . . . it isn't hard to guess. Not after what he did to me."

"Tell me," I gritted out.

She stared at the floor, unblinking. "He took everything. Our house. Our things. Anything of value he sold and kept every dime for himself, pissing it away. And we moved into this shitty trailer where Clara and I shared a bedroom and a bathroom, both with doors that didn't lock."

My spine went rigid and my heart pounded. "Aria, I won't make you go through this. If you don't want to talk about it—"

"No. You were right. And you should know."

"Are you sure?"

She gave me a sad smile. "I haven't told this to anyone. Ever. Only Clara knows."

They'd survived it together.

"It was fairly miserable for five years. That's about how long it took Craig to run out of money. He literally just . . . spent it. He gambled. He quit his job. He threw parties while Clara and I hid in our room and prayed no one came in. He was such a loser, but there was always food and he normally left us alone."

"You were ten."

She lifted a shoulder. "Old enough to care for ourselves and get to school."

Meanwhile at ten I'd had a full staff of private teachers at my disposal. And parents and grandparents. Yes, they'd been on the opposite side of the country, but had I called, they would have sent a plane.

"By the time we turned fourteen, things started to get strange. Craig would look at us. He'd lick his lips and there'd be this gleam in his eyes as we started to develop breasts. Girls know when a man is staring. One night, Clara woke up to see him standing over her bed. After that, we hung a can on the door so we'd hear if he came in. After about a year, it became so bad—the looks and long touches—that we started packing."

"To run away."

She nodded. "There was this girl who lived in the trailer park, two trailers down. Londyn."

"Cadillac Londyn?"

"The same. Her parents had been junkies, so she was on her own too. One day she was just gone. We started asking around at school and the pizza parlor where she worked. No one knew she was living in the junkyard, just that she was hanging out there. But we figured that was where she was staying too. And if it was good enough for her, it was good enough for us."

A junkyard wasn't good enough for her, but it was better than the alternative.

"We didn't leave right away," she said. "We stole some money from Craig and bought the biggest backpacks we could find. Then we filled them to the brim with clothes and food and cash and Tylenol. We'd planned to take twice as much as we actually did but things . . . well, things got out of hand."

My pulse pounded at my temples, fury coming on before she could explain.

I knew what was next. The question was, just how out of hand had it gotten?

"We waited one night too many," she whispered. "I was in the kitchen, making dinner. Macaroni and cheese. I didn't even know he was home, but then I felt him. He came up behind me and . . ."

I took her hand.

She laced her fingers through mine and held tight. "He touched me."

With her free hand, Aria touched her breast. Then lower.

I wanted to scream. I wanted to punch the wall and kill a man in Temecula, California. But I sat still and let her squeeze my hand so hard that my fingertips turned white. Tomorrow, I'd take it out on my heavy bag, but tonight I was here for Aria.

"He kept touching me. He ripped my shirt. He got my pants open. I fought, hard, and stomped on his foot. It was enough to squirm away and run to our room. It happened so fast, Clara barely registered what was happening when I came racing down the hall. After that, we barricaded ourselves in the bedroom. We sat against the door, wedging ourselves between it and one of the beds. He beat on that door for hours, until our legs were so weak they shook and the tears had dried on our cheeks."

At fifteen. *Fuck.* They had to have been terrified.

"We waited for hours after his footsteps retreated from the door, just in case. Then when we were sure he was gone, we pushed every piece of furniture against the door. By morning, we'd shoved the backpacks and supplies out of the tiny bedroom window, then squeezed out ourselves."

All these years I'd known Aria. All these years I'd worked with Clara. And I hadn't really known them at all.

Aria's strength was humbling.

"Clara and I walked hand in hand to the junkyard, and that was it," she said. "We found the delivery truck and made it our home. We did what we could for money until we were old enough to get jobs. We stayed far away from the school and the trailer park. If we saw someone we knew, we didn't tell them where we were living because we were all scared the cops might stumble upon our makeshift home and take us away. By some miracle, it worked. We survived. Together. The six of us leaned on each other. And we survived."

Aria. Clara. I'd underestimated them both.

Later, when my temper had cooled, I'd find out about the uncle. I'd find out if he was still alive. I wasn't going to ask if she'd kept tabs on the motherfucker.

"I'm sorry." I kissed her knuckles. "I don't . . . I don't know what else to say."

"There's nothing to say. It's in the past. I want it to stay in the past."

"Then we won't talk about it again."

"Brody . . . the cradle. The nanny. You do it because you want to help. But I need to earn things. I need to know they are mine."

"They are yours."

"No, they're not. They're gifts."

"What's wrong with gifts?"

She stared at me, searching for the right words. When she found them, her gaze softened. "I went for so long wondering what was going to happen. I have spent so long relying only on myself."

"And now you have me."

"Brody, I know this seems strange. I know Clara can take a gift and say thank you. I can't."

"Why?"

"Because tomorrow it might be gone. If I earn it myself, then maybe it won't disappear."

In that single sentence, it all made sense. She was

protecting herself. She was insulating herself from heartbreak. If she counted on me and I left her . . . "I won't leave you, Aria."

"You might."

"Never."

Not when I was falling for her.

She closed her eyes and collapsed into my chest.

I wrapped my arms around her and kissed the top of her hair. "I'll always take care of you. Let me. Please."

"Make me a part of it. Share it. Please?"

"Okay." I kissed her hair again, holding her for a few precious minutes. Then I stood from the bed, her dainty hand tucked firmly in my grasp. "Come on."

Aria stood too. "Where are we going?"

"Dinner. Bed."

"Not yet." She dropped my hand to snake her arms around my waist. Her fingers dove into the back pockets of my jeans and she squeezed my ass. Hard. "Did you wear these jeans because you thought it would make me less angry at you?"

"Maybe. Did it work?"

She stood on her toes and her lips whispered across mine. "I guess you'll find out when you take them off."

CHAPTER FOURTEEN

ARIA

"Courtland."

"I will never, ever name my child Courtland."

Brody frowned. "That was my great-uncle's name."

"Did you love and admire this uncle?"

"I didn't really know him."

"Then it's a no." I took a bite of my cheeseburger and scrolled down the list of names I'd been collecting on my phone. "Parry. Spelled with an *a*."

"Meh."

That made five in a row he'd nixed with a *meh*. Ben. David. Steven. Jacob. They'd been too plain. And now Parry. "Fine. Your turn."

Brody and I had been making lists of baby names. We'd collect favorites throughout the week, then have lunch at the flower shop on Fridays to pitch them to each other. Today he'd come bearing cheeseburgers from the diner because it was the one craving I'd had consistently during the transition from the second trimester to the third.

In the past month, ever since I'd confided in Brody about my past, the two of us had settled into little routines, like this one. Dinner every evening. Breakfast after he'd worked out in the morning. Texts throughout the day to check in. Saturday night dates in the theater room. Anything to spend time together.

Today we were debating boy names. Next week, we'd start tackling the girl list.

"Adler," he said.

I scrunched up my nose. "Adler?"

"It was my grandfather's name."

"It's not awful. But it's . . ."

"Pretentious?" Brody finished.

I pointed a finger at him. "Now you're learning."

He chuckled and wadded up the paper wrapper from his meal. "What if we can't agree?"

"We have three months. I'm sure we'll find one boy name and one girl name that we both like."

"I think you underestimate our natural tendency to disagree."

I giggled and tossed my napkin at his face.

The smile on his made my heart flip.

I'd seen that smile more in the past month than in all the years I'd known Brody. Even Clara had commented on how happy he was.

How happy we both were.

We bickered endlessly about stupid topics like nursery purchases and the BMW I wouldn't drive. Every time I lifted an object weighing more than two pounds, Brody would scold me for five solid minutes.

The arguments, I was learning, were foreplay. Because by the time each day closed, we would be together, either in his bed or mine, and there was never any argument about ending the night naked and wrapped in each other's arms.

"I brought cookies too." Brody pulled another to-go container from the white paper sack on the table.

Before he'd arrived at noon, I'd cleared away the floral petals, leaves and discarded stems from the bouquet Marty had made for one of five deliveries we had today.

"Can I run an idea by you?"

"Of course," he said.

"You have to promise not to run out and spend a bunch of money."

He frowned. "Have I bought you anything extravagant lately?"

I tore off a chunk of cookie and popped it into my mouth. "This cookie is fairly extraordinary."

He grinned. "Your idea."

"Someday, in the distant future when I'm ready, I want to build a greenhouse. I love working with the flowers and making bouquets. It's been an exciting change from what I did in Oregon, but I miss playing in the dirt. I can grow houseplants for the shop and maybe even expand to have annuals and perennials available to customers."

"I like it. Whatever you set your mind to, I have complete faith you'll make it a success."

"Thank you." I blushed and tore into the chocolate chip cookie, moaning as the sugary, buttery confection melted on my tongue. The greenhouse idea wouldn't be anytime soon. I needed to save some money and get the shop turning a bigger profit, but someday, I wanted both.

"Marty's going to have to run the shop this afternoon," I said, devouring my cookie. "I'm going to be in a food coma."

"I heard that." Marty walked into the room with a grin on his face. "And I'll allow an afternoon nap if you agree to call the Friday promotion Fresh Flower Friday."

"Done." I clapped. "Easy."

That was my favorite name out of the options anyway. But if I could get a nap in on the gold velvet couch in the office, I was taking it.

"See how easily some people can agree on names?" I shot Brody a smirk.

He simply shook his head. "Eat your cookie."

"Yes, sir." I winked and took a huge bite to polish it off.

Fresh Flower Friday was going to be a new addition to Welcome Floral. We were going to rearrange a wall just inside the door. We'd add shelves to hold tin buckets.

Then each Friday, we'd fill them with bundles of fresh flowers and offer them at cost.

The goal was to get people into the shop. For too long, Welcome Floral had survived on deliveries to area residents. That would always be our core business, but to expand, we needed foot traffic.

When John Doe drove home from work, we wanted him to stop here and grab a bundle for his wife, Jane, who'd had a long week. We wanted Jane to then come in and shop for a birthday gift for her mother.

Over the past month, we'd rearranged the shop. The tables had a better configuration to showcase not only the floral arrangements, but also the houseplants and knick-knacks and gifts. The shabby-chic style had been toned down, the clutter cleared and the lights brightened to give the shop a clean and open look.

It still had charm and character. But individual pieces were given space so they could breathe. The layout didn't overwhelm the eye, but showcased items so customers could appreciate the beauty of a clay planter or a lawn ornament or a succulent terrarium.

The door dinged, and when I made a move to stand, Marty held up a hand. "Sit. I've got the shop."

"Thanks." I smiled at his back as he disappeared from the workroom. Then I rubbed my belly. I might have gone too far with lunch. I was stretched tight. "Ready?"

Brody inched closer, putting both hands on my rounded stomach. After every meal, the baby would kick for a few minutes, sometimes longer. Brody was on a mission to feel as many as he could.

The black-and-white-striped tank top I'd worn this morning stretched tight across my abdomen. I'd finally had to give in and buy maternity jeans. Today I'd rolled up a dove-gray sweater and knotted it at my ribs, over the bump.

Brody and I were color coordinated today, him in a light-gray suit. He'd even traded his normal dress shoes for sneakers. They were new and perfectly white, but they were casual. And he'd left his normal tie at home.

"Come on, little one," I whispered. "Kick Daddy for wanting to name you Adler and Courtland."

Brody laughed and leaned in to kiss my forehead. "You're such a smart-ass."

"You like it."

"You're right." He put his forehead to mine and we both waited, our breaths held, until one tiny baby foot slammed into Brody's palm. "That never gets old."

"No, it doesn't."

"I've got to get back to work."

I'd see him in hours, but I always hated to watch him walk away. "I know."

I was so in love with him.

The realization had snuck up on me this morning when he'd curled his strong, tall body around mine. He'd held me and I'd realized that the soul-deep loneliness I'd felt for years had truly vanished. Not even Clara's hugs or August's cheek smooches had chased it completely away.

Only Brody.

And our baby.

I loved him, more than I'd ever known it was possible to love another person.

Soon, I'd find a way to say the words. But in this moment, as the three of us huddled together in a bubble away from the real world, I closed my eyes and savored the moment. The peace.

The bubble popped before I was ready.

"Sorry to interrupt." Marty poked his head into the room. He was grinning from ear to ear. "We've got some guests. Friends. I'd like you to meet them."

"I better get back to work anyway." Brody lifted his hands and framed my face. Then he dropped a soft kiss to my lips. "Don't work too hard."

"I won't." I slid off my stool and took his hand. "Will you take a plant with you? We got the coolest snake plant in this morning and I decided to steal it for the entryway."

"There are already seven pots in the entryway."

"Your point?"

He fought a smile, then looked to Marty. "Don't let her lift anything heavy. Yesterday, I caught her trying to move a—what kind of plant was that?"

"A fiddle-leaf fig tree."

"A tree. She was trying to move a tree."

"It wasn't heavy."

Brody's expression flattened. "Ask Marty for help."

"She won't have to," Marty declared. "I won't let her out of my sight."

"Good." Brody took my hand and together we followed Marty into the shop. The easy grin on his face faltered and his feet skidded to a halt when he spotted the older couple inspecting the shop.

"Ned. Stephanie. I'd like you to meet Aria Saint-James." Marty introduced me to the couple. "Aria, Ned and Stephanie Backer. Former owners of Welcome Floral."

"Oh." I stood a little taller and extended a hand. "Hello. It's so nice to meet you."

Because Brody had bought the shop from them, I'd never known their first names. Marty didn't talk about them much, but when he had, he'd referred to them as the Backers. Never Ned and Stephanie.

"You too." Ned took my hand, shaking it with gusto. "It's just a pleasure."

Stephanie simply smiled, her eyes wandering around the room. "You've made a lot of changes."

"We have." I held my breath, hoping they wouldn't take offense. "I truly love this space."

Ned turned to Brody and extended a hand. "Mr. Carmichael. Nice to see you again."

"A pleasure." The easy posture from lunch was gone. Brody stood stiff, his face drawn tight.

"What brings you to town?" Marty asked, leaning

against one of the display tables. "Judging by your Instagram photos, I figured we'd never get you back from Hawaii."

Stephanie laughed. "We love living there. It's so green and wonderfully humid. My skin has never felt better."

"We're back for John Miller's sixtieth birthday," Ned said. "Then we'll fly home."

"It's been lovely to see you." Brody gestured for the door. "May I escort you out? We'll let Aria and Marty get back to work."

The smiles on Ned's and Stephanie's faces dropped.

I shot Brody a scowl. Why was he being rude? "No, please. Stay. We're not that busy. And you should catch up with Marty."

"Are you sure?" Stephanie asked me, giving Brody a cautious glance.

"Yes, it would be wonderful. Please."

"Thanks." She relaxed, taking another gander around the room. "We've missed this place. We ran this shop for twelve years. It was sort of like our third child."

"A third child who actually made us money." Ned barked a laugh. "I don't see Suzie or MJ selling for four hundred and eighty thousand dollars. Not that we'd ever sell our kids."

Stephanie laughed. Marty laughed.

Brody tensed.

And my jaw dropped.

Four hundred and eighty thousand dollars.

It was tacky as hell for Ned to announce that number. And enlightening.

"You said one hundred and twenty-five," I whispered, looking up at Brody.

His eyes were on the door, like he wanted Ned and Stephanie gone. Now I knew why he was so eager to shove them onto the sidewalk.

Except the damage was done. They'd spilled his secret.

"You said one hundred and twenty-five," I repeated, crossing my arms over my chest.

He dropped his gaze to meet mine and there wasn't an apology on his face. No, there was only guilt.

Tension settled like a black cloud in the room, thickening the air so much it was hard to breathe.

"Say something," I demanded.

He blinked, then looked over my head at Marty. "Would you please excuse us?"

Brody didn't wait for Marty's reply. He gripped my elbow and led me back through the workroom and into the adjoining office, closing the door behind us. It was a small room, taken up mostly by the wooden desk and couch. But there was just enough floor space for me to put a good three feet between us.

"How could you?"

"Aria, let me explain."

"Why? It seems fairly clear. You bought the flower shop for a half a million dollars—"

"Not quite that much."

"Details," I hissed. "Half a million dollars, then lied to me about the price. Why?"

"Because there's no need for you to be saddled with an enormous debt. Not when I can afford it."

"It's not about the money!" I shouted, my voice bouncing off the walls. "You came to Oregon and told me you had a flower shop. Did you?"

His silence was the only answer I needed.

It slashed through my heart. It nearly dropped me to my knees.

All this time and I'd had such faith that Brody had always been honest. What else had he lied to me about?

"You lied to me."

"I had to."

I shook my head. "No, you didn't. I would have moved. Without the flower shop, I still would have moved."

"I couldn't take that chance." He waved to my belly. "I needed you here."

And I would have been here. Simply because he'd asked to be involved in our child's life. But he hadn't given me that chance. He hadn't given me his trust or his faith.

My chin began to quiver as my eyes flooded with hot, angry tears. Goddamn hormones. They were stealing my edge. "I am so mad at you right now. You don't get to decide the course of my life. You don't get to keep secrets from me. You've had months to tell me the truth. Months."

"We didn't think it was worth upset—"

"We?"

Brody flinched, realizing he'd just fucked up.

"Clara. She knew."

He closed his eyes and nodded.

"Get out." I turned my back to him before he could see the first tear fall.

"Aria—"

"I said get out."

He stood there, for minutes, waiting. But when I didn't turn, he blew out a long breath and left.

It wasn't until the door's bell jingled that I breathed. Then I let myself cry the unshed tears, for just a moment, before pulling myself together and wiping my face dry.

Nothing good came from crying. I'd learned that after my parents had died. Clara and I had been ten when our parents had been stolen from us. The pain never did go away. It had dulled with time, but like the junkyard, it was unforgettable.

Rivers of tears hadn't brought them back to life. Rivers of tears hadn't kept my uncle away. Rivers of tears hadn't saved me from living in a junkyard at fifteen.

Tears were pointless.

Tears wouldn't make Brody change.

Dirt. "I need dirt."

I needed work. So I stormed out of the office to find Marty alone in the shop, a look of worry etched on his face.

"Are you—"

"I'm fine." I marched to one of the pots that we'd ordered a few weeks ago. I'd left it empty because it would need the right plant. Well, that snake plant was it.

There was no use taking it to Brody's home. There was no use making myself comfortable there when I couldn't possibly stay. Not now. I'd let myself get swept away with the idea of *what if*.

This baby didn't need a mother with her head stuck in romance novels. It was time for a reality check.

I wouldn't stay with a man who refused to *listen* to me. I wouldn't live with a man who didn't *respect* why I needed to control my own destiny.

After all I'd confided in him, all the pain I'd dredged up so he could understand. He still hadn't told me the truth.

That hurt the worst. In all the nights he'd held me in his arms, he hadn't found the courage to admit he'd lied.

The tears threatened to return but I blinked them away. Then I crouched, ready to haul the pot to the back room, when a sharp zing raced through my abdomen.

"Ow!" I cried, letting go of the pot as I clung to my belly.

"What?" Marty was at my side in a flash.

"I don't know." I gripped his arm, using him for balance. "It hurts. Just . . . give me a second."

"What are you doing lifting that?"

"It's not heavy." It wasn't heavy. Maybe ten pounds.

I'd put it in this very spot just three days ago. "It's not heavy."

"Breathe." He clutched my arm, just as another pang raced through my side. The pain was so sharp, it was like someone had hold of my stomach and was ripping it in two.

"Ah!" I gasped, dragging in some air. *Please, let the baby be okay. Please. Please. Please.*

"Aria, what do I do?"

I met his worried gaze. "Take me to the hospital."

CHAPTER FIFTEEN

BRODY

"Aria Saint-James." I braced my hands on the counter as the nurse behind it looked over the rim of her clear-framed glasses.

"She's my sister," Clara blurted from beside me. "We're family."

The nurse opened her mouth, but before she could speak, Marty rushed to my side.

"Brody." His face was pale. A sheen of sweat clung to his bald head. "She's down here."

Clara and I followed him, the three of us jogging down the hospital hallway, dodging carts pushed against the walls and a wheelchair outside of an open door.

When Marty reached Aria's room, he stood aside and let us rush in first.

Aria was in the narrow bed, her hair draped over her

shoulders. Her hands rubbed circles on her belly, and when she spotted Clara, the worry lines on her forehead relaxed. She spared me a brief glance.

She was pissed. She had a right to be. But I didn't care.

I rushed to her side and took her hand.

She ripped it free.

"Are you okay?" I asked.

"I'm okay."

"The baby?"

"Fine." She sighed and focused on her sister as Clara sat on the opposite side.

"What happened?"

"I was at the shop and I bent to pick up a pot."

"You should have let Marty—"

She shot me a glare so pointed that it shut me up. "It wasn't heavy. I lifted it three days ago."

I would still be having a word with Marty about what Aria lifted at work.

"I got these sharp pains." She ran a hand over her stomach, indicating the spot. "It freaked me out, so I had Marty bring me here. The doctor said it was round ligament pain."

"Is it serious?" I asked.

Aria shook her head. "No, it's normal. The round ligament just got stretched too far and too fast when I moved."

"Good." Clara sighed. "When Marty called . . . God, you had us worried."

When Marty had called, I'd nearly come out of my skin. I'd never driven so fast in my life. Clara had barely hopped into the passenger seat before I'd sped away from the house.

I'd gone home after Aria had kicked me out of the shop. Work had been pointless, and what I should have done was stay there and watch over her.

"How long do you need to stay?" I asked.

"The doctor said I could go home soon. The nurse was here a few minutes ago. She said they're getting my discharge papers ready."

"Okay. Then what?"

"Rest." She lifted a shoulder. "It will go away. If it doesn't, then I need to come back."

Clara leaned in and pulled Aria into a hug. "Are you okay?"

"I'm okay." Aria closed her eyes and wrapped her arms around Clara. "It scared me."

Scared was too mild a word. Terrified. Panicked. Those weren't right either.

Never in my life had I felt such a deep, endless fear. If Aria had been hurt. If the baby . . .

They were my life. Both of them.

Aria was my heart.

"Can we have a minute?" I asked as Clara let Aria go.

"Sure." She gave me a sad smile, then kissed her sister's forehead. "I love you."

"Love you too. Later we're going to talk about you

keeping secrets from me. You know, like how much the flower shop actually cost."

Clara cringed. "You found out."

"I found out."

"Sorry. You can yell at me later. For now, I just want you out of this hospital."

"You and me both," I muttered.

Clara slipped into the hallway where Marty hovered. When the door closed, I sank to the edge of the bed.

Aria turned her gaze to the wall.

"I'm sorry." I clutched her hand with both of mine. "I'm sorry, baby."

"You should have told me about the shop."

"Yes, I should have told you."

She slumped deeper into the bed. "We can't keep doing this. Having the same argument. My heart can't take it, Brody. I think . . . maybe this was never going to work."

"Don't."

"This was about the baby. You know that if I wasn't pregnant, we never would have gotten together. I think we need to call this what it is. We're trying to make something that isn't meant to be."

Aria was giving up on me.

She was giving up on us.

But there was so much to fight for. Too much to lose the battle of my lifetime.

I refused to let her give up.

"I met Heather at a party."

That won her attention. She turned away from the wall to face me.

"It was a company Christmas party. She came as the date of one of our employees. She left with me." Maybe that was why I hadn't been truly shocked when she cheated with Alastair.

"Why are you telling me this?"

So she'd understand something I'd realized earlier today when she'd kicked me out of her flower shop. Something I suspected Clara had figured out a long, long time ago and was the reason she'd never objected to my gifts.

She'd known why.

"Heather and I dated for a while, then she started to hint at wanting a ring. I bought one. I gave it to her. I didn't even ask. One day, she didn't have a ring. The next, she did and she could tell everyone she was engaged to Brody Carmichael. That's all she'd really wanted. Bragging rights."

Heather had cared more for my name than she had for me. And I hadn't really cared at all. She'd been a companion. I hadn't had to search for dates for company functions or business meetings. She was beautiful and absent.

That was what I'd liked best about Heather. She'd left me alone to do my work. She hadn't bulldozed her way past my guards like Aria, not that Heather would have stood a chance.

She wasn't Aria.

"I didn't buy her things," I said. "Yeah, I got her

birthday and Christmas gifts. I'd pay for a vacation. But otherwise, she was on her own."

Heather had begun to resent me when I hadn't let her move into my place. While the rest of her friends who'd landed rich fiancés had been able to quit their jobs, Heather had needed to keep working.

When Alastair came around, she must have seen him as her ticket to financial freedom.

All she'd had to do was time it so that I'd catch the two of them in bed. Heather had to have known that Alastair would want her simply because it had been another way to one-up me.

"I don't understand," Aria said. "You didn't buy her things?"

I shook my head. "No."

"Why?"

"Because I didn't love her."

Aria's mouth fell open. "What?"

"My parents. My grandparents. They didn't hug me. They didn't tell me they loved me. I watch you and Clara together and it's . . . I never had that. When I was a kid, my birthday meant a mountain of gifts, all wrapped and purchased by my mom's assistant. The nanny watched me open them. When I turned sixteen, my grandfather had a car sent to my school. They bought me things."

"That's not love, Brody."

"Isn't it? Because that's the only kind of love I know."

Aria shifted, sitting up straighter. "Not anymore."

239

"No." Not anymore. I tucked a lock of hair behind her ear. "I love you. Damn, but I love you, woman."

"And that's why you buy me things."

I nodded. "That's why I'll try to stop."

She stared at me, those mesmerizing eyes glassy with tears. "I love you too."

I closed my eyes and let the words sink past the skin and into my heart. Had anyone ever told me they loved me? I think Heather had, probably before she'd asked for something. Maybe my mother, a long, long time ago.

They'd been empty words.

From Aria, they were magic. They were the future.

I leaned down, dropping my forehead to hers. "It was never about the baby."

"Sure it was."

"No." I shook my head. "I fell in love with you the moment you stole that vase of flowers."

"They were really pretty flowers." She let out a quiet laugh and the sound filled my chest so full I could barely breathe.

"I love you," I whispered.

"You said that already."

"It's worth repeating."

She took my face in her hands, her thumbs stroking my beard. Then she pulled my lips down to hers, kissing me with so much tenderness and promise, I knew that for the rest of my life, I'd hold on to her. Above all else, Aria was the endgame.

"Take me home," she said against my mouth.

"I'll go find the doctor."

An hour later, after one last check from the doctor and a string of nurses bearing pamphlets on pregnancy—the Welcome hospital was nothing if not thorough—Aria was home. Clara had ridden to the shop with Marty to pick up the Cadillac.

"I think I'm going to lie down." Aria yawned as I led her inside.

"Good idea. Your bed? Or mine?"

"Mine's closer."

"How about tomorrow we pick one and just call it ours?"

"Deal. As long as you let me pay for the entire flower shop."

"No." I shook my head as we walked into the bedroom. "It's not worth that price."

"But you paid it anyway."

"For you? I'd buy the moon."

"Brody, this is . . . it's too much. You know why it bugs me."

I led her to the bed and pulled back the covers. Then after she slid beneath the sheet, I settled in behind her, holding her close. My hands rested on her belly, hoping to feel the baby kick just to be sure he or she was okay.

A little tap. That's all I got. But it was enough.

"I'm not going anywhere, Aria. I have all this money. What's the point of it if that means we struggle?"

"The struggle is what affirms you're alive. Without it, the bright moments don't shine."

"How about a compromise?"

She twisted to look at me. "I'm listening."

"You'll pay the one twenty-five for the shop. And you agree to drive the BMW. It's safer than the Cadillac."

"Do you actually understand what compromise means?"

I chuckled. "Shh. Listen. I'm getting to the part you're going to like. In exchange for that, I won't buy you anything new for six months."

"Twelve."

"Nine."

"Twelve. And once that time is up, we'll put a limit on the size of future gifts."

"Christ, you are stubborn."

"Then it's agreed." She gave me a smug grin. "A year. And a limit."

"A year," I conceded. "And a limit. But items for the baby don't count."

"Agreed." She nodded and snuggled deeper, then drifted off to sleep.

I waited for an hour or so, watching before slipping out of the room. When I went to my office, it was no surprise to find Clara there. She'd canceled my last meeting of the day and rescheduled those I'd missed.

"I'm just about done here," she said. "I need to get

August from preschool. Do you need anything before I go?"

"No. I'm not doing much." My concentration was shit and I wanted to be close when Aria woke up. "I'm not working tomorrow. Or Sunday. You should take them off too."

"That's the plan. I've got a date with my main man for a bike ride and picnic."

August was a lucky kid to have her as a mom. And my child would be lucky to have her as an aunt.

"I'm not good with sentiment."

"Really?" she deadpanned.

"Your sarcasm has really blossomed since Aria moved here."

She laughed. "What can I say? She brings out the best in people."

"She really does. I just . . . I wanted you to know that you don't owe me anything. For the house here or anything. I didn't buy them out of charity. I don't want you to feel obligated or indebted or—"

"Brody." She cut me off and smiled. "I know. This isn't necessary."

"You work hard."

"I'm grateful for all you've done for August and me. But that's not why I work hard."

"You're sure?"

"I promise."

I sighed. "I'm glad I'll have you as my sister."

Her eyebrows rose. "Sister?"

"If she'll have me."

Clara rushed me for a hug. It was short but strong, and when she stepped back, she pressed a hand to her heart as her eyes lit up. "Thank you for loving Aria."

"I will until the day I die."

"I know." Tears flooded her eyes as she waved goodbye, leaving me alone in the office.

After an hour of returning emails, I went to see if Aria was still asleep, but when I walked into the room, the bed was empty and the patio doors open.

"There you are." I found her wrapped in a blanket, standing beside the pool. Her eyes were cast to the horizon. "What are you doing out here?"

The sun was slowly setting and the temperature dropping. Even though it was spring, the nights were cool.

"I like the sunsets here." She leaned into my side. "In a way, they remind me of the sunsets we used to watch at the junkyard. When you don't have TV or video games or smart phones, you look to the world for something to watch. I've missed that since leaving. I haven't appreciated the world enough."

I guess that was true for all of us. So we stood together, watching as the colors shifted. When a layer of orange coated the sky, I dug the ring that I'd pulled from the safe earlier out of my pocket.

"Aria Saint-James?"

"Yes, Brody Carmichael?"

I grinned and turned her to face me. Then I dropped to a knee, the ring in hand. "Marry me."

"W-what?" She did a double take at the five-carat Harry Winston.

"Will you marry me?"

"Seriously? You just promised two hours ago not to buy me anything for a year."

"I said anything new. This isn't new. I've had it for a week."

She blinked. "You have?"

"Can we focus, please? I asked you a question."

"I kind of like seeing you on your knees."

I shook my head and the ring. "You're impossible."

"Someone has to keep your ego in check."

I chuckled. "You're doing a damn fine job at the moment. You're shredding it to pieces here, baby."

"We can't have that." She touched a fingertip to the ring and smiled. "Yes. I'll marry you."

I surged to my feet and sealed it, crushing her to my chest as I swept my tongue into her mouth. Mine. She was mine. From now until forever, the one thing in this world not for sale was the best gift of my life.

She laughed, breaking the kiss. "That ring is too big."

"You'll get used to it."

Aria leaned into me. "I love you."

"I love you too." I kept her in my arms as we faced the sunset again. "What do you think? Want to stay in Arizona? Or go back to Oregon?"

"Arizona is growing on me. And besides, it's where the Cadillac brought me."

"So?"

She tipped her chin up and smiled. "You can't argue with that Cadillac."

EPILOGUE

ARIA

Three months later . . .

"Drive safely."

Clara nodded and slammed the trunk of the Cadillac. "I will."

August was buckled into his car seat, his legs bouncing wildly as he waited for them to get on the road.

"Call when you get to Phoenix." I pulled her in for a hug.

"Okay. We're going to swim and relax tonight. Then Elyria tomorrow." Her voice shook as she clutched me tight.

"Are you sure about this?"

She let me go and squared her shoulders. "I need to do this. And it's my turn in the Cadillac."

The car gleamed cherry red under the bright and

beautiful Arizona sun. I'd miss it. That car had brought me to the home I hadn't realized I'd needed.

"Be careful," Brody told her.

"We will." Clara stepped closer, giving him a sideways hug as she touched the baby's foot. "You two try and rest. I know it's hard when they are so little. Take naps whenever you can."

Here she was worried about Brody, me and our five-day-old newborn son. We'd be fine. Tired, but fine. It was her I was worried about.

Clara had finally planned her trip to California. She'd waited until the baby was born and probably would have waited longer, but with August on summer break, it made sense for her to go while things at work were quiet. Brody's paternity leave meant Clara wasn't needed in the office all day.

And when she'd asked Brody for a week off, he'd encouraged her to go. We both had. My sister needed this trip, not only for a vacation with her son, but also because the longer she waited, the longer the car sat in her garage, the more anxious she became.

After twelve years away, Clara was facing old demons. At least she'd have August, her little pillar of strength, with her on the way. And the car. There was courage in that car.

The Cadillac was finally returning to California.

To Karson.

"We'll be back soon." She forced a smile and went to

the driver's side door. She patted her pocket where she'd tucked a note with Karson's address.

Years ago, before she'd started her own journey in the Cadillac, Gemma had hired a private investigator to track all of us from the junkyard down. When we'd had our latest book club virtual chat, she'd told us that she'd had the PI confirm Karson's address, not wanting to send Clara to the wrong place. It was a good thing too since Karson had moved to a new town.

Elyria, California. A small town on the coast known for its surfing and loving community. Elyria.

All of us—Londyn, Gemma, Katherine, me—were excited for Clara. Karson had been the glue who'd held us together at the junkyard. He'd discovered it, made it a home, and kept that home safe for the rest of us. If he wasn't doing well, if his life had fallen apart . . .

It would break our hearts.

Clara's especially.

I'd cautioned her to expect anything, to be prepared for the worst, but she'd insisted it would be fine. She was eager to see him for herself.

"Bye." She pulled me into one last hug, then got in the Cadillac.

My heart crept into my throat as the engine rumbled to a start and the wheels inched forward, picking up speed as she drove down the lane.

"She'll be okay." Brody put his free arm around my shoulders and tucked me into his side.

"I hope so." As the Cadillac disappeared, I leaned into Brody's strong body, using it for support. And yawned.

"What about Danny?" he asked.

"Boring." I yawned again.

"What about Adl—"

"If you suggest Adler one more time, I'm going to the courthouse tomorrow and putting Parry, with an *a*, on his birth certificate."

Brody frowned and let me go. Then he retreated with the baby into the house, passing the plethora of plants I'd added to the entryway. After some paint and colorful toss pillows and throws, this concrete house was coming to life. He carried the baby into the bedroom and carefully set him in the cradle at the foot of our bed.

"He's five days old," he said. "My son needs a name. Adler's not that bad."

"Look at him." I tossed up a hand. "Does he look like an *Adler*?"

The name made me cringe. Probably because Brody kept suggesting it. If I actually thought he loved the name and was paying homage to his late grandfather, I would have caved. But even he didn't like it much. It was just at the top of his mind.

Much like Parry, with an *a*.

Neither of them was the right name. None of the countless other options we'd debated were either. The baby name book that rested on my nightstand had a hundred pages dog-eared, but no matter what we threw out there, nothing fit.

Our son had arrived five days ago after thirteen hours of labor. He had gray eyes that I hoped would become Brody's green. He had a mat of dark hair and the cutest nose on earth. He was the center of our universe.

And damn it, he had to have the perfect name.

"Come on." Brody took my hand and pulled me to the bed. "We're exhausted. Let's just . . . lie down for a few minutes."

"Why does he only sleep during the day?" I collapsed onto the mattress.

Brody did the same, facing me as we both relaxed into our pillows. He stretched one hand across the tiny space between us and took mine, bringing it to his lips before closing his eyes.

The black T-shirt stretched across his broad chest was fresh, as were his gray sweats. It wasn't entirely fair that he looked gorgeous after a ten-minute shower. Meanwhile I'd taken a thirty-minute bath and blow-dried my hair in an attempt to feel human again but still looked like I'd been trampled over by a herd of dirty zebras.

"Brody?"

"Hmm."

"I love you."

"I love you too, baby." Those words never got old. "Rest."

I closed my eyes but my mind refused to shut down.

This was the most exhausted I'd ever been in my life, but there was daylight beyond the blinds and my brain wouldn't shut the hell up.

Name. We needed a name.

What kind of mother couldn't think of a name for her baby? We'd run through the entire list of family names on Brody's side and mine. None fit. Clara had already named August after our dad so that wasn't an option.

Why couldn't we come up with something? Why wasn't it bothering Brody more? Didn't he care about our baby? Didn't he want to get this right? Clearly not if he could just lie there and fall asleep in five seconds flat.

"Brody."

He didn't stir.

"Brody."

Nothing.

"Brody." I yanked my hand from his grip and poked him in the ribs.

He gasped awake, snapping up to look at the baby. "What? What's wrong?"

"We need a name."

He groaned and face-planted into his pillow. "Aria, he doesn't need a name this second."

"What kind of parents are we that we can't give him a name?"

"The indecisive kind." Brody reached for me, inching close. Then with my hand firmly in his once more, he held it to his heart. "We're the kind of parents who love him so much that we're not rushing a decision he'll live with his entire life."

I sighed. "I hate it when you win our fights."

"Were we fighting?"

"In my head."

He chuckled and scooched close to kiss my forehead. "Sleep. I don't want you worn out."

"Too late."

"Close your eyes." The command was meant for me, but he obeyed it himself. Those eyelashes fluttered shut.

I counted sixty-three sheep and still hadn't drifted off. "Brody."

He answered with a snore.

"Brody," I whispered.

Brody.

Like the man, I loved the name. It was pretentious and arrogant. It fit him perfectly because he was both of those things. And loving. Generous. Kind.

Never in my life had I felt so cherished than when I was with my husband.

Brody and I were married not long after he'd proposed. We didn't invite anyone but Clara and Marty. August was Brody's best man. Ron, a man who never stopped surprising me with his hidden talents, performed the ceremony on the patio at sunset.

No fuss. No party. No expenses besides my dress, and since Brody hadn't been able to buy it for me thanks to our purchasing armistice, I'd bought it myself. A long-sleeve, ivory tulle gown with lace on the bodice and wrists. The empire waist had showcased my belly, not hidden it away. Three hundred bucks and a floral arrangement from my own shop.

With the sunset at our backs and Brody impeccable in a tux, it was the second most special day of my life, eclipsed only by the day our son was born.

Brody.

That was his name. Brody. After a father who had been fighting for him since the beginning. After a father who'd rather die than miss a day of his life. After a father who loved him and his mother with every beat of his heart.

"Brody." I poked him again.

This time he just opened his eyes and glared. "Sleep."

"I want to name him Brody, after you."

He blinked, coming awake and shoving up to his elbow. "After me?"

"Yes. Brody Carmichael Jr."

"Actually. He'd be the third. Dad's name was Broderick."

"It was?"

He nodded and yawned. "His family might not be as wealthy, but they are just as pretentious."

Brody didn't speak much of his parents. Of any of his family, really. Alastair hadn't contacted him once, not even bothering to reply to Brody's email that we'd gotten married. Coreen had done her best to disown Brody and would have if not for business. She was still throwing a tantrum and making threats to sell Carmichael Communications, but Brody had called her bluff and she hadn't had the gall to see it through.

He was simply enduring her fits until his birthday this fall.

Then he would be free.

Once he was in control of Carmichael Communications, he'd pursue the best deal possible to sell the company. There were already options being discussed in secret, but at the moment, everything work related was on pause while we adjusted to life as parents.

"Brody Carmichael the Third." I smiled at the rush of adrenaline that shot through my veins. *Brody Carmichael the Third.* "I don't hate it."

"Me neither." He grinned. "We could call him Trace."

"For the Third." *Yes. Yes. Yes.* "That's it. Trace."

"Trace." Brody's smile widened. "We'll go to the courthouse tomorrow. Now will you go to sleep?"

"Yes, sir." I closed my eyes and snuggled into his arms. Thirty seconds later, a whimper came from the cradle. The baby was hungry. Nap time was over.

So Brody and I both roused.

And introduced our son to his name.

―――――

THE RUNAWAY SERIES concludes with Dotted Lines.

ACKNOWLEDGMENTS

Thank you for reading *Forsaken Trail*! This series is such a joy for me to write and I am so grateful for my readers.

Special thanks to my editing and proofreading team: Elizabeth Nover, Julie Deaton, Karen Lawson and Judy Zweifel. Thank you to Sarah Hansen for the cover.

A massive thanks to my reader group for your love and support. I couldn't have dreamed up a better team of super fans. Thank you to the incredible bloggers who read and help me with promoting new books. I am so grateful for all the work you do to support me and the romance community.

And lastly, to my friends and family. Thank you!

ABOUT THE AUTHOR

Devney Perry is a *Wall Street Journal* and *USA Today* bestselling author of over forty romance novels. After working in the technology industry for a decade, she abandoned conference calls and project schedules to pursue her passion for writing. She was born and raised in Montana and now lives in Washington with her husband and two sons.

Don't miss out on the latest book news.
Subscribe to her newsletter!
www.devneyperry.com

Made in the USA
Coppell, TX
29 April 2024

31862616R00156